- Keeping a butterfly in captivity is like trying to control your own destiny. Both will eventually die from exhaustion.

Al Smith

Death of a Butterfly

- The screenplay -

To be released as a major motion picture

Purpix Media Corp.

Purpix Media trade paperback 2nd edition April 2010

Text set in Courier New.

Book Editors
Eileen Dennie
Tishia Smith
Anthony Davis
Monique Taylor
Lolita Smith
Michael Taylor

Manufactured in the United States of America
Copyright Registration: Pau 3-372-218
ISBN: 978-0-578-03441-6

Acknowledgements

First and foremost, I thank the Lord for planting this seed in me to develop such a story.

I would like to say thank you to my mother and father, Lolita and Leal Smith Sr., my brother Jerrell and his wife Tracie for always being cheerleaders. I also would like to acknowledge and show gratitude to my extended James family, Robert "Pops, "Floretta, Bobby, Sheronda and family, and Chaleta and family. I have a total of 46 uncles and aunts (some deceased) and so many cousins that I don't know how many I truly have. They all have encouraged me one way or another. I would like to say a special thank-you to Michael Taylor and to my cousin Anthony Davis for calling me frequently to ensure that I complete this screenplay.
A sincere thanks goes to Aunt Marilyn for praying for me and calling to give me encouragement and inspiration. Thank you! To my family at Trinity CME, I say "thank you." To Pastor Walker and my Abundant Life Family in Atlanta, Georgia: I greatly appreciate the nurturing of my spiritual growth. Many thanks goes to my new church family, New Life Community Church (Indianapolis, IN), and Pastor Hunt. To Jason Steiner: I greatly appreciate your creative input on the cover design!

To the fellas—Michael Taylor, Anthony Davis, Robert Smith, Dion Gartin, George Powell—and all the families associated: This one is for the crew!

(left to right) Leala, Tishia & Lynnette

To my family,

    I dedicate this book to my wife, Tishia, the love of my life. And I also dedicate this to my two little princesses Lynnette & Leala. The thought of expressing my love for you in words would be an injustice. I thank all three of you for enriching my world and allowing me to enjoy the beauty of the simple things in life.

    To Lynnette & Leala – May both of you grow in the Lord and your lives be filled with good health and full of joy. I pray that both of you stay close to one another and keep God's love in your hearts for the rest of your days.

– Aka-Daddy 09

Death of a Butterfly

LEGEND

Cont'd:	Continued dialogue from previous page
INT:	Interior scene (inside of a building, home, etc.)
EXT:	Exterior scene (outside)
V.O.:	Voice over

EXT. DOWNTOWN ATLANTA - DAY (PRESENT DAY)

The city, Atlanta, is revealed in the background.
A butterfly floats down toward the buildings below.
The butterfly swoops down toward the street and
lands on a picket sign held by a protester. The
signs they carry read, "Black women, not Black
hoes" and "Jazzy-belle."

The butterfly invades a protest of angry, old church
folks. The butterfly becomes annoying and one of the
protestors sways it away toward onlookers, which
includes a much younger age group.

The younger group finds the protestors hilarious
and feels that they are wasting their time. One of
the onlookers has a little girl. The little girl
becomes intrigued with the butterfly and tries to
catch it with her hands. In the pursuit of the
butterfly, she runs out in the street and is barely
missed by a car from the oncoming traffic.

The girl is instantly grabbed and removed from
oncoming traffic by her mother. The mother's
reprimand is harsh. It is not clear what is said
to the daughter.

The butterfly continues to fly throughout the crowd
and dashes up to one of the office windows in the
building. This window looks into the office suite
of a well-known record label. Inside this office
stands a 40-year-old, thin, white male, the CEO.

While looking down at the protestors, he is joined
by the company's attorney.

INT. RECORD LABEL OFFICE SUITE - DAY

                    ATTORNEY
          So what's next? They've been
          out there for three days now.
          You gotta say something.

The CEO paces back and forth, thinking.

                      CEO
          No. Not really. Bad publicity
          is still publicity.

He pauses.

                      CEO
          Each day they stand out
          there, it's that much more
          attention my business gets,
          free advertising.

                    ATTORNEY
          I don't understand the big
          deal. Just don't put her in
          the videos anymore. Or if
          you do, make sure she has
          clothes on.

                      CEO
          Stick to what you do. Law is
          yours. Selling music is mine.
          You make it seem like your
          suggestion is a quick fix.
          Jazmyne has boosted Yadeh's
          popularity big time. He alone
          has had the most web hits on
          any internet site since the

                         CEO (Cont'd)
          internet was invented.
          One billion hits. One billion.
          Do you know how many people
          that is? That is bigger than
          a presidential election or the
          OJ trial. Web hits translate
          to dollars from our partners.
          Let'em march…I'm a businessman,
          not a minister.

EXT. DOWNTOWN ATLANTA - DAY (SAME DAY)

A news reporter stands outside the building with
the protestors.

                         NEWS REPORTER
          We are coming to you live from
          122 Peachtree Street in downtown
          Atlanta, where protestors have
          gathered together to address the
          issue of how Jazmyne Greer, one
          of the nation's most popular
          video dancers, portrays women in
          a negative light. Protestors have
          been out here for days and are
          pretty upset with what has taken
          place at this record label. They
          are taking a stand to stop this.

The news cuts to a series of interviews from people
on the scene.

                         OLDER BLACK WOMAN
          This has to stop today. Today.
          Long have we let this nonsense
          go on. Long have been the days

                    OLDER BLACK WOMAN (Cont'd)
          where we let our little girls—
          that's what they are, little
          girls—do this. She could be
          my daughter.

                    PASTOR
          I don't think that they realize
          what they are doing is eternal.
          Every action has a consequence.
          They just don't see it right now.

                    YOUNG BLACK MALE
          Man, she is just doing her
          thing. People want to hate
          on her because she looks
          good. I mean.

                    NEWS REPORTER
          Do you think that it's
          appropriate, what she's doing?

Scene cuts to a montage of pictures of Jazmyne cir-
culating on the internet, with a caption that reads
"May be inappropriate for small children."Most of
the pictures have areas of her body blurred out.

                    YOUNG BLACK MALE
          I mean, if people don't like
          it, don't watch it. Plain
          and simple.

EXT. RURAL GEORGIA - DAY

Butterflies are being released at a wedding.
Children are playing and there is so much laughter
and love in the air. An older black male, better
known as Papa, helps one last butterfly out of the
box. He was hired to release butterflies at the
wedding once the ceremony was over.

                    PAPA
          Go on, little fella, I know
          you can do it. Yeeesssss!
          Yeeesss! (Says with great
          intent)

The last butterfly staggers but finally makes it out
of the box and flies away.

The camera pans through the crowd and follows
the children at play. The camera slows down to a
girl dancing in front of an overweight boy taking
pictures of her with a Polaroid camera. He loves
taking pictures. And she loves being in front of
the camera.

                    JAZMYNE
          Make me gorgeous, Joshua.

                    JOSH
          I'm tryin', I'm tryin'!

Papa is ready to leave and begins to call the young
girl's name.

                    PAPA
          (from a distance) Jazmyne!
          Jazzy! Jazzy!

The little girl stops dancing because she hears Papa. The little boy wants to impress her with his picture, but the picture takes too long to develop. He fans and shakes it as fast as he can but it is too late. He runs behind her then stops and waits for the picture to develop. It is a work of art (He stops in front of the camera).

                    PAPA
          Come on, child. When you hear
          me calling you, I expect you
          to come on the first time,
          not the fifth.

                    JAZMYNE
          Yes, Papa.

                    PAPA
          Now help me gather up these
          boxes. We gotta go.

EXT. FRONT PORCH - NIGHT

An older 2-bedroom house in the middle of the country is filled with aging pictures, old television sets and old gadgets, which are no longer used. They are dusty and tarnished.

Papa is sitting out on the front porch humming an unidentifiable song. Jazmyne goes out to the front porch. She should be in bed.

                    PAPA
          Child, you done gone crazy?
          What you doin' up?

Jazmyne shrugs her shoulders.

> PAPA
> Nightmares again?

Jazmyne nods her head and sits in his lap.

> PAPA
> You know what I do when I
> have nightmares?

> JAZMYNE
> What, Papa?

> PAPA
> I blink them away. I keep
> blinking and soon they are
> all gone.

They continue to sit silently.

> JAZMYNE
> Papa, what do you do out here
> all the time?

> PAPA
> It gives me time to think
> back over my day. We had a
> good day today, didn't we?

Jazmyne nods.

> PAPA
> The wedding was beautiful.
> The bride was really pretty,
> wasn't she?

Al Smith

Jazmyne nods again.

                    PAPA
          She was almost as pretty as
          you are. (touching her nose)

Jazmyne smiles. There is a moment of silence
between the two.

                    JAZMYNE
          You think I'll ever get
          married, Papa?

                    PAPA
          Pretty as you are? If I
          wasn't so old, I'd marry you
          myself! (chuckling)

                    JAZMYNE
          Papa, that's nasty. You are
          my Papa.

                    PAPA
          When the time is right, I'm
          sure you won't have no problem.
          Yes, when the time is right.

INT. INNER CITY PROJECT APARTMENT - DAY

The room is filled with many people, loud voices,
cigarette smoke, and alcohol. There is a card game
taking place with "Rapper's Delight" playing on the
television in the background.

One woman in particular gets real excited about the
song and gets up and begins dancing.

                    LAYLA
          Oh, that's my song right there.
          That's what they call rap, girl.
          This is it…

Several other women join her in dancing. Layla
glances over to her husband, an up-and-coming
minister.

                    LAYLA
          Not bad for a janitor's wife,
          huh?

Everybody starts laughing.

                    LAYLA
          I'll show you somebody who
          can jam. Yadeh, get on out
          here, boy.

She runs in the back room and comes back with a
five-year-old boy. Still sleepy he tries to get his
bearings straight. He slowly gets into it. And
before long he is seriously into the music.

                    LAYLA
          That's my baby. Do it, baby!
          Do it, baby! Hey!

4 HOURS LATER

The apartment is a pure mess. All of the company
has gone and Layla and her son, Yadeh, are passed
out on the living room sofa. The sound of the
television is down but there are color bars
showing. The man tries to wake his wife up by

Al Smith

shaking her, but she is in a stupor. He picks her
up and takes her to their bedroom and comes back
for their son. It's amazing that no one is awakened
by his noisy, clanking key chains on his belt.
He begins picking his son up, but in the process
begins fondling him. Yadeh wakes up and begins
fighting with him, begging him to stop.

                    YADEH
          What are you doing? Please stop,
          Daddy. Daddy! (crying)

INT. SCHOOL CLASSROOM

                    TEACHER
          Everyone, go ahead and pass
          your homework up to the front.
          And don't forget about the
          school talent show tonight.
          Who is performing tonight?
          Raise your hand.

Several students raise their hands.

                    TEACHER
          Celeste, what are you doing?

                    CELESTE
          I'm singing a song.

                    TEACHER
          OK. Peter, what are you doing?

                    PETER
          Karate.

                    TEACHER
          Ooh, sounds exciting.
          Jazmyne, what are you doing?

                    JAZMYNE
          Dancing.

                    TEACHER
          I can't wait to see all of you.
          Josh and you?

Before Josh can speak another kid speaks out.

                    KID ONE
          Eating!

The entire class starts laughing.

                    TEACHER
          Who said that? Who said that?

No one comes forward. The teacher becomes
agitated at this point because no one raised
their hand.

                    TEACHER
          Fine. Since no one wants to say,
          everyone pays. Extra homework.
          And you can thank the comedian
          for it later. Everyone open your
          history book to page 325. Do
          the review questions at the
          bottom of the page. Due tomorrow.

EXT. NEIGHBORHOOD STREET - DAY

Al Smith

Jazmyne and Josh are walking home with some of the other neighborhood kids. Josh is always the center of ridicule because of his weight.

                    JAZMYNE
          So what song do you want to do?

                     JOSH
          I was thinking…

                    KID ONE
          (Interrupts) Little pig, made
          us get extra homework.

                     JOSH
          Huh?

                    KID ONE
          You heard me, little pig and
          bug girl. You and that stupid
          camera!

                    JAZMYNE
          Shut up. It was your mouth that
          got us in trouble.

The kids start shoving Josh around, and they are about to jump on him. Jazmyne drops her book bag and balls up her fist.

                    JAZMYNE
          Stop it. Before I lay all
          ya'll out.

                    KID TWO
Oooh, bug girl is going to
beat us up. Where is your
crazy-ass granddaddy and his
bugs to save you?

The five kids start laughing and begin
surrounding them in a circle. All of the kids
hesitate but KID TWO. He steps forward and punches
Josh in the mouth. Josh drops his camera and the
lens cracks. His face follows his camera and hits
the ground as well. All of the kids start yelling,
"Fight, fight, fight."

Jazmyne watches the fight for a second but doesn't
like what she sees. Josh swings and misses, swings
and misses. Josh can't fight and is getting beat
up! She steps in and punches kid two to the ground
then swings her book bag around and grazes kid one.
By this time, there is a nice-size crowd circled
around the activity. The five kids decide to leave
them alone and leave the circle.

                    KID THREE
        Little pig and bug girl.

                    JAZMYNE
        (to Josh) You OK?

                    JOSH
        They were gonna really beat us
        up, huh?

                    JAZMYNE
          Nah, they are some sissies.
          I always gotchya back, Josh.
          We are the dynamic duo. I
          gotta teach you how to fight.
          You missed both swings. That's
          not good. Did you even try
          to duck?

She wipes the blood off his forehead and they share
a moment of eye contact. He then reaches down to
get his camera.

                    JAZMYNE
          You more worried about your
          camera than you are about
          your face.

Josh picks the camera up and looks at the lens,
looks at Jazmyne and catches up with her.

INT. ELEMENTARY GYMNASIUM

The talent show is taking place and there is not
a lot of talent in Americus, GA. Many of these
children have no singing or dancing ability, until
Josh and Jazmyne get to the stage. They electrify
the crowd.

                    TEACHER
          We'd like to thank all of the
          parents for coming out and the
          faculty who worked so hard to
          put this event together.
          The last act we have tonight is
          Josh Shepherd and Jazmyne Greer.

                    TEACHER (Cont'd)
          They go by the name of the
          Dynamic Duo.

Josh walks out on stage first in a tight, grey,
shiny suit. The stage is empty, except for a
microphone stand. He looks at the audio man and
signals for him to push on the tape. A praise
and worship song comes on and he begins singing.
Jazmyne joins him after the music starts. She is
dressed in a white and pink ballerina outfit. She
performs a praise dance and the audience really
begins to get into it. They bring the house down.

EXT. OUTSIDE OF A FUNERAL HOME - DAY

CG: 12 YEARS LATER

A funeral has just taken place and Papa was hired
to release butterflies. He asked Jazmyne to help him
with the job. She agrees but unwillingly.

                    PAPA
          Make sure that all of the
          butterflies have left the boxes.

In all the boxes, Jazmyne half looks around and
ends up kicking one.

                    PAPA
          Look, I don't care if you're
          mad at me. Couldn't really
          care less. You ain't going to
          that party. I don't know them
          folks and it just don't sit
          right with me.

                    PAPA (Cont'd)
          I don't know that boy either.
          He has yet to come and meet me.
          That raises a red flag right
          there. So that's that. I'm
          tired of talkin' bout it now.

                    JAZMYNE
          But Papa, Andre just isn't
          some boy. He's, he's….

                    PAPA
          I don't care if he's Action
          Jackson, we're done talking.
          Get the boxes and come on
          or there will be another
          funeral than…

Papa picks up the obituary and reads the name.

                    PAPA
          …Oscar Dozier today.
          You got that?

Jazmyne begins picking up the boxes and glass jars,
folding them up and putting them in a trash bag.
She notices that there was one butterfly stuck to
the bottom of a carton. She looks around to see
if anyone is looking. It is still alive. It is a
different color than the other butterflies released
earlier that day.

EXT. RURAL GEORGIA (1970s) - DAY - FLASHBACK

Jazmyne and Papa are out in the field of pink
lilies playing with his butterfly net. Jazmyne
catches a butterfly and shows it to him.

                    PAPA
          Do you know what type of
          butterfly this is?

She shrugs her shoulders "no."

                  JAZMYNE
          A pretty one.

                    PAPA
          Yes, it is. (laughing) This is
          a Monarch butterfly.

They both look at it for a brief moment.

                    PAPA
          Alright, it's time to cut
          him loose.

Jazmyne shrugs her jar to the other side of
her body.

                    PAPA
          No, child, as pretty as they
          are, they must always be let
          free for the Lord. They
          represent the soul. If you
          keep it…you never want to
          keep it. You always want a
          free soul, don't you?

                    JAZMYNE
          No, I want to keep my soul.

                    PAPA
          (talking to himself) My child
          trying to keep your own soul.
          Trying to control your own path
          is the devil's form of slavery.
          Always let your soul go to the
          Lord. In order to truly live,
          you first must let go. Your life
          is not your own, my child.
          It's God's.

EXT. OUTSIDE OF A FUNERAL HOME - PRESENT DAY

Jazmyne puts the carton in her purse. She then
continues to clean up like nothing ever happened.

INT. INSIDE JAZMYNE'S BEDROOM - LATER THAT DAY

Jazmyne sits on the bed and pouts for not being
able to go to the party. She mumbles to herself.
Papa walks in.

                    PAPA
          I need to run to Piggly Wiggly
          to get some pizza sauce. I'll be
          right back, OK?

Jazmyne is silent.

                    PAPA
          I said,OK?

                    JAZMYNE
          OK! (sarcastically)

                    PAPA
          Thank me later. If Action
          Jackson really likes you,
          he'll be around. Don't rush
          into nothin'. Listen to me now;
          believe me later on…in
          the future.

Papa exits the room and leaves the house. Jazmyne
looks out of her window to see him pull out of
the driveway and drive down the street. She goes
back to her room, opens her bag, and looks at the
butterfly that is stuck to the box. It is still
alive and attempts to fly but is stuck to the box.
She closes the box and goes into the kitchen and
looks for an empty jar. She sees some grease
sitting on the kitchen counter. The label on the
jar reads "fish grease." She empties the jar down
the sink and rinses it out. She then takes the
jar back to her room and transfers the butterfly
from the carton to the jar. She watches the
butterfly fly around in the jar (very close to her
face). She puts the jar down on her chest of
drawers. She pouts for a second and walks around
the house aimlessly. The doorbell rings, and she
thinks its Papa. She walks to the door and proceeds
to open it.

                    JAZMYNE
          You forgot your wallet,
          didn't you?

Al Smith

She is startled when she realizes it is Andre.
She is totally caught off guard.

> ANDRE
> Ready to go?

Jazmyne looks around and pulls him inside.

> JAZMYNE
> Boy, you gon get me in trouble.
> What you doin' here?

> ANDRE
> You told me to hook up with
> you at the party.

> JAZMYNE
> That didn't mean to come to
> my house. My grandpa will kill
> you if he catches you here.
> You gotta go.

> ANDRE
> Oh, you trippin'. Come on,
> let's go. He'll just put you
> on punishment.

Jazmyne pauses.

> JAZMYNE
> You gotta go. He'll be back
> any minute. I do want to go but….

> ANDRE
> But what? Come on. Come with me.

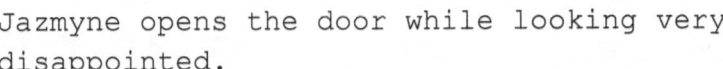

Jazmyne opens the door while looking very disappointed.

> JAZMYNE
> Bye, Andre. I'll see you at
> school on Monday.

> ANDRE
> (pauses) Aight, I'll see
> you later.

He gives her this look like "you messed up."

Jazmyne closes the door extremely upset.

She begins pacing around the room and is very upset. She begins crying and then gets completely angry. She turns her stereo on and plays Public Enemy's "Rebel Without a Pause" as loud as she can and begins throwing things and tearing up her bedroom. She moves over to her mirror and begins changing her look.

DANCE MONOLOGUE

Her hair color changes, her complexion is lighter. After her transformation, she begins cleaning up her room and takes the butterfly that she caught earlier that day and puts it high on the shelf in her closet.

INT. HIGH SCHOOL HALLWAY - DAY

Jazmyne and her friends are walking down the hallway talking about the talent show that evening.

                    GIRL ONE
          What did ya'll do in
          Mr. Smith's class?

                    GIRL TWO
          A surprise quiz on chapter 8.

                    GIRL ONE
          I swear that man has nothing
          to do but punish us for not
          havin' no woman at home.

                    GIRL TWO
          It was easy. It was from last
          night's homework.

                    JAZMYNE
          Homework?

                    GIRL TWO
          See...that's why you on the
          five-year plan.

Andre and his buddies walk past. He and Jazmyne
catch eye contact. She stops him to talk but he
looks disinterested.

                    JAZMYNE
          I'll talk to ya'll later.
          (talking to her friends)
          What's up? Why you ain't call
          me back? (to Andre)

                    ANDRE
          I had to help my mother fix our
          fence in the backyard.

                    JAZMYNE
        All night?

                    ANDRE
        I had homework!

                    JAZMYNE
        You coming tonight to see me
        and Josh perform?

Andre is looking around.

                    ANDRE
        I don't know, I might.

                    JAZMYNE
        You might?

Jazmyne finally turns around to see what he is
looking at, and it's another girl standing right
behind her. The bell rings.

                    GIRL
        Hey, Jazz. Andre, we're about
        to be late.

Jazmyne moves aside and lets Andre leave with the
girl. Another girl walks up to Jazmyne and they
walk to class.

                    GIRL TWO
        Come on, girl; let's get ready
        for the quiz. Don't sweat it.
        She's a hoe anyway. She just
        did it with three guys from the
        basketball team at that party

                    GIRL TWO (Cont'd)
          last weekend. I think you know
          one of'em.

                    MR. SMITH
          Glad you two could make it!

Mr. Smith waits until the two girls enter his
classroom and he closes the door.

INT. HIGH SCHOOL AUDITORIUM - NIGHT

Josh is waiting back stage for Jazmyne to show up.
He's forced to go on by himself because he and
Jazmyne are the last act to perform.

Jazmyne is walking through the hallway toward the
dressing room back stage to prepare for her and
Josh's performance. She passes one of the doors
where the auditorium is and she peeks in to see
everyone in attendance. She sees Andre in the crowd
and they catch eye contact. She sees another girl
is with him. She gives a motion to come where she
is. She does it discretely so that his date doesn't
see her. He looks around and whispers to his date
that he is going outside for a minute. He
immediately gets up and leaves.

He meets Jazmyne behind stage. They stare at one
another, and begin kissing. Jazmyne becomes extremely aggressive. He pushes back a little, but
let's Jazmyne proceed forward. One thing leads to
another very quickly.

INT. HIGH SCHOOL AUDITORIUM

TEACHER
Alright, everyone. They've been
performing at all of Americus'
talent shows since I can remember.
Here to make their final
appearance before they graduate,
give it up for the Dynamic Duo.

Josh walks out on stage and looks a little nervous.
He does no introduction but commences to sing "I
Surrender All."

Half way through the song, Josh is emotional, a
spotlight appears behind him and Jazmyne glides
across the stage and begins dancing.

Her entrance ignites the audience and they stand to
their feet. His song and her dance together make a
beautiful performance.

They bow at the end and proceed off stage. Andre is
waiting back stage to greet Jazmyne. Josh is taken
off guard by Andre's presence.

ANDRE
Baby, that was awesome.

JOSH
(looking confused) That was
different. I thought you was
going to stand me up, like you
did for prom.

JAZMYNE
Easy, cowboy, I made it.

                    ANDRE
        What's up, Josh?

                    JOSH
        Andre, why you backstage?

                  JAZMYNE
        This is my new beau.

They hug and give each other a small kiss.

                    ANDRE
        Look, baby, I gotta split.
        I'll talk to you later.

                  JAZMYNE
        OK, call me later.

Andre looks at Josh with a quirky smirk and leaves
backstage.

                    JOSH
        So when did ya'll become
        an item?

                  JAZMYNE
        Today.

                    JOSH
        Interesting. You know that?

Josh peeks through the curtain from backstage and
sees Andre holding hands with the girl he came
with. Jazmyne doesn't see them.

Papa walks up and interrupts their conversation.

                    PAPA
          You guys make me so proud.
          I'm telling you.

Jazmyne looks at him with a fake smile and gives
him a hug.

                    PAPA
          Dinner is on me tonight.
          Where you two want to go?

Josh and Jazmyne look at each other and smile.

INT.SOUL FOOD RESTAURANT - NIGHT

Josh, Jazmyne, Papa, and Mrs. Shepherd, Josh's
mother, sit at the table and talk about the other
performances.

                    JOSH
          Did you see Lisa's outfit?
          Did she have on any clothes
          or was that paint?

Josh and Jazmyne laugh.

A group of kids walk up to the table and give
compliments to Josh and Jazmyne.

                    STUDENT
          That was all that! Ya'll did
          a good job.

                    JOSH
          Thank you!

Al Smith

Josh looks at Jazmyne and she turns around and smiles at the students. Silence overcomes the table. Mrs. Shepherd and Jazmyne catch eye-to-eye contact.

                    MRS. SHEPHERD
          You look different. I noticed
          that you changed up your hair.
          But something seems different
          about you? What's different?

Jazmyne's body language shows that she is uncomfortable with how the conversation is going.

                    JAZMYNE
          Nothing. I changed my clothes
          up a little. Nothing drastic
          though.

Papa sees that Jazmyne is uncomfortable and tries to change the subject.

                    PAPA
          So what's next, kids? This
          is it. The Dynamic Duo will be
          going separate ways. It has
          been really fun, Norma,
          hasn't it?

                    MRS. SHEPHERD
          Yes, it really has. Both of
          you have been such a blessing.
          Jazmyne, you have been like a
          daughter to me over the years.
          I feel like you are one of
          my own.

                    JOSH
         Don't let Sheila hear you
         say that!

Everybody laughs out loud.

                    JAZMYNE
         We all know how Sheila feels
         about me.

                    MRS. SHEPHERD
         She likes you. She just has a
         funny way of showing it. You
         know how she is. She's like
         that with everyone!

The laughter comes to an end, and a moment of
awkward silence comes over the party. Papa brings
the conversation back to where the two were trying
to avoid.

                    PAPA
         So...what's next? Graduation is
         a couple of weeks away. Jazmyne
         has been keeping it hush hush.
         Seeing she has it all planned
         out, I let her do her thing.
         So let's start with you, son.
         (looking at Josh)

Josh is a little uncomfortable and moves around in
his chair.

                    JOSH
        Well… (looks at Mrs. Shepherd)
        I am planning on working for
        about a year to save up some
        money to go to art school up
        in Atlanta. You know how I love
        this camera. I can't picture
        myself doing anything else.

                MRS. SHEPHERD
        And where you plan on working?

                    JOSH
        I don't know, somewhere.
        You need help with the bills.

                MRS. SHEPHERD
        Child, don't let me be your
        crutch. I will be just fine.
        Child, I want you to fly. I
        won't be your excuse. You are
        scared. Admit it.

Everybody laughs and he nods his head in agreement.

                    JOSH
        Yeah, a little. I'm not ready
        to leave just yet.

                MRS. SHEPHERD
        Alright, but do note, you ain't
        staying in my house forever.
        You have got to fly someday.

                    JOSH
        Yeah, I know.

Another awkward brief silence comes over the party
and everybody looks at Jazmyne. She is drinking
water and almost chokes. She is fishing for some
words to say.

                    JAZYMNE
          Well, I ain't scared.

Everybody laughs.

                    JAZMYNE
          No, for real though. Uhm,
          I applied to Julliard to dance.

The party is amazed.

                    JAZMYNE
          And if that doesn't work out,
          I'll try a couple of schools
          in the area and go there in
          the fall.

                    PAPA
          You know...

Jazmyne bows her head in embarrassment.

                    JAZYMNE
          Oh, here we go!

                    PAPA
          Shut up. (laughing) I'm serious.
          You have been such a blessing
          to me. You have really grown up
          to be a beautiful woman.

                    PAPA (Cont'd)
        When Lisa decided to leave,
        I really didn't know what I
        was going to do. But I prayed
        to the Lord that He give me
        the strength and the will to
        see you through. I thank Him
        every day for you. I know I'm
        not your father, but you have
        been more of a daughter to me.
        And I know things haven't been
        good between us all the time,
        but I thank you for sticking
        in there with me. I was going
        to wait until graduation to
        show you this, but I had to do
        it tonight.

He pulls out an envelope, with a local bank logo on
it and gives it to Jazmyne.

                    PAPA
        Read the statement.

Jazmyne opens the letter and reads the balance
statement.

                    JAZMYNE
        It's a bank statement.

                    PAPA
        Keep reading.

                    JAZMYNE
        $20,000? You kiddin' me?

                    JAZMYNE (Cont'd)
This has my name on the account.
Papa, you kiddin' me! What's
this for?

                    PAPA
You. Your future. College.
I didn't want money to be an
excuse for you.

Josh looks happy but jealous. Everybody seems very
happy.

                    JAZMYNE
Oh, Papa, I can't think of
nothing to say. I know that
I don't deserve it.

INT. CLASSROOM - DAY (TWO WEEKS AGO)

                    HIGH SCHOOL COUNSELOR
Jazmyne, we've tried to help
you as much as we could but
you had to help yourself first.
You know that you don't have
enough credits to graduate this
year, right? Why didn't you go
to summer school?

Jazmyne avoids eye contact and talks under her
breath.

                    HIGH SCHOOL COUNSELOR
Speak up? I didn't hear you.

> JAZMYNE
> I'm sure that there is
> something that you can do?

> HIGH SCHOOL COUNSELOR
> Like what? Give you the credits?

> JAZMYNE
> Can I do extra credit in some
> of those classes or something?
> I'll do anything. Please?

Jazmyne reaches her hand out and rubs the
counselor's leg with a sexual undertone. The
counselor looks at Jazmyne eye-to-eye and slowly
pushes her hand off of his knee.

> HIGH SCHOOL COUNSELOR
> As pretty as you are, LITTLE
> GIRL, even you have to have
> the minimum requirements to
> graduate. I get one of you
> every year thinking that
> offering me sex will help
> them graduate. The names
> change but the circumstance
> is always the same.

Jazmyne begins to cry. She regains her composure.
She looks at him and begins to seduce him. He pulls
back but doesn't stop her.

INT.SOUL FOOD RESTAURANT - NIGHT (PRESENT DAY)

> JAZMYNE
> Thank you, Papa. I love you.

                    PAPA
      You are more than welcome, dear.

They hug and she tears up.

INT. YADEH'S BEDROOM - LATE EVENING

Yadeh has got headphones on and is listening to
some type of hip hop music but it is not clear what
song. He is in a serious creative moment. His
mother comes in and tries to get his attention.

                    LAYLA
        Yadeh.

Yadeh cannot hear because his headphones are
extremely loud.

                    LAYLA
          Yadeh! (yelling)

Yadeh jumps because he is scared by her presence.
He turns off the radio.

                    YADEH
        Yeah, Ma.

                    LAYLA
        What are you doing?

                    YADEH
        Nothing.

He slides his journal behind him.

                    LAYLA
          You be off in your own little
          world writing. Look, I'm about
          to run to the store. I need you
          to clean the kitchen so I can
          cook when I get back. Your father
          just got off a cleaning job.
          He just fell asleep, so keep
          it down.

Yadeh looks sad to hear the news.

INT. YADEH'S FAMILY KITCHEN

The family kitchen has mountains and mountains
of dishes. In addition to the dirty dishes is an
infestation of roaches. Yadeh has never been used
to sharing space with these pests. To make himself
comfortable in the surroundings, he brings his
radio into the kitchen and begins cleaning up.

He begins getting into the music, "Parents Just
Don't Understand," and he turns his music up a
little more. It becomes so loud that his father
gets up from the couch and makes his way toward the
kitchen. His heavy key chains weigh down on his
belt. He startles Yadeh by stopping the music.

                    JAMES
          Boy, did your mother tell you
          that I was trying to take a nap?

                    YADEH
          Sorry. (turns around to continue
          to clean the dishes)

JAMES
What I tell you about playing
the jungle bunny music in
my house?

YADEH
It's not jungle bunny, rabbit
whatever music, "Parent's just
don't understand?" Come on.

JAMES
You talking back?

YADEH
No. (Yadeh becomes scared.)
I'm sorry.

Yadeh's father walks toward him.

JAMES
What you 'pologizin' for then?

His father begins pushing him around. The pushing
turns into fondling.

YADEH
Stop. Please stop. What kind
of father are you?

They begin wrestling and the last comment made his
father furious. They continue to wrestle and the
wrestling turns into a fistfight. They begin tearing
up the kitchen and breaking dishes. His father
manages to take his key chain off his belt and
swings it at Yadeh. He manages to cut Yadeh's face
in three places just below his right eye.

During this commotion, Yadeh's mother comes into the house and tries to break up the fight only to be hit by one of Yadeh's loose punches. He knocks her down to the ground. The fight immediately stops.

YADEH
Momma, I'm sorry. Are you OK?

LAYLA
(crying) Why are you fighting?

Yadeh tries to explain but is cut off because Yadeh's father doesn't want her to hear about how he has been molesting him.

JAMES
Shut up! We are tired of you.
Get out. Get out now. Go.

Yadeh regains his composure and grabs his things out of his bedroom and leaves. He and his father catch eye contact one last time before he leaves. Yadeh has a napkin over the cut on his face.

LAYLA
James, don't do this. It was
a mistake. He didn't mean to
hit me.

JAMES
Layla, I'm tired of this.
Boy, get out! Now!

Fade to black.

INT. HIGH SCHOOL HALLWAY - DAY (GRADUATION DAY)

Josh is talking with some of his buddies in the
hallway as they line up to their seats in the
auditorium. As their conversation continues, Josh
sees Jazmyne walk by crying. He immediately pulls
her off to the side.

                    JOSH
          What's wrong?

Jazmyne continues to cry but says nothing.

                    JOSH
          What's wrong?

Jazmyne continues to cry.

Josh tries to figure out what's wrong but comes up
without answers. Finally, he sees Andre
snuggled up with another girl up against a locker.

Josh proceeds to confront Andre for breaking
Jazmyne's heart. Josh taps Andre on the back.

Andre turns around to see who it is and then shrugs
his shoulders to proceed to kiss on the female.

                    JOSH
          I really got to speak with you
          right now.

Andre continues to shrug Josh off.
Josh gets frustrated and swings at Andre. Andre
dodges and comes back with a punch to the stomach.
Josh stunned by the punch, staggers, recovers, and

Al Smith

charges toward Andre again. By this time there is a small crowd around the fight.

They begin circling one another and Josh swings, misses, and Andre comes with a severe punch to the stomach, then another to the face. This combination totally puts Josh out of commission. Andre proceeds to punch on Josh while he is down on the floor.

Jazmyne breaks through the crowd and pushes Andre off Josh.

                    ANDRE
          You crazy trick. I told you
          that it was over so you had to
          bring your fat friend to get
          with me? You lucky it wasn't you.

                    JAZMYNE
          I hate you. I hate you!

Jazmyne proceeds to pick Josh up off the floor.

                    JAZMYNE
          You really have to stop doing
          this. If you start a fight,
          I need you to at least win.

They look at each other and start laughing.

                    JOSH
          I got a couple of extra programs.
          You get one?

Josh hands Jazmyne a program and she begins looking though it while they walk down the hallway.

Papa is wandering through the halls trying to find out where to sit. He passed all of Jazmyne's classmates.

> PAPA
> Excuse me, hi. Do you know Jazmyne?

> GRADUATE ONE
> Yeah, I know her.

> PAPA
> Have you seen her?

> GRADUATE ONE
> Yeah, but I haven't seen her today.

> PAPA
> Thank you, son.

Papa continues to roam aimlessly, trying to find a familiar face and he runs into Mrs. Shepherd.

> PAPA
> Hey, Norma.

> MRS. SHEPHERD
> Hey, how you doin'?

They hug.

> PAPA
> Alright, just tryin' to find my child. You seen Jazz?

                    MRS. SHEPHERD
          Well, I sure haven't. Hmm.
          Josh is behind the stage. I'm
          sure she's with him.

Both walk back to where Josh is. Josh sees them
and looks sad. He knows that they are looking for
Jazmyne.

                    MRS. SHEPHERD
          Have you seen…Man, what
          happened to you? You get in
          a fight or something?

                    JOSH
          I had a minor accident.

                    MRS. SHEPHERD
          Minor? You OK?

                    JOSH
          I'm good.

                    MRS. SHEPHERD
          We'll talk about this later.
          You seen Jazmyne?

                    JOSH
          Yeah, I saw her earlier.
          We were looking through the
          program, she didn't see her
          name, and so she got up and
          left. She came back and gave
          me this.

Papa becomes worried.

JOSH
          She told me to give it to you
          if she didn't see you before
          the ceremonies.

Mrs. Shepherd and Papa look at each other confused.
He takes it from Josh and opens it up.

<Pomp & Circumstance music begins playing>

He begins reading the letter and stops. He covers
his mouth and begins weeping. He leaves the area
and continues crying while he reads the letter.

                    JAZMYNE'S V.O.
          Papa, I don't know how to even
          begin telling you this, but I
          am not graduating today. I'm
          sorry. I know that I am letting
          you down big time. You just
          seemed so proud of me at the
          restaurant that I just didn't
          want to let you down. You have
          sacrificed so much for me my
          entire life and the one time
          for me to make you proud, I
          make myself a big embarrassment
          to you. I don't want to be like
          my mother. Please forgive me.

Classmates are walking across the stage getting
their diploma and shaking hands with the teachers
and administrative staff.

EXT. OUTSIDE FRONT OF THE HOUSE

Al Smith

Jazmyne packs up her car and takes off down the street.

                    JAZMYNE'S V.O.
          I've decided, instead of
          bringing more embarrassment
          to you, I should leave. As of
          today, I am out of your house
          and will make my own way. I will
          call you when I get settled.
          There is one thing that is true
          from our conversation. I am not
          scared to fly. I will be a
          professional dancer. I will make
          you proud of me. And I will
          graduate with my high school
          diploma. Please don't worry,
          I will be fine.

Love always, Jazmyne.

INT. HIGH SCHOOL HALLWAY (GRADUATION DAY)

Papa walks down the hallway crying as the announcer proceeds to announce names.

CG: 2 YEARS LATER

INT. GEORGIA STATE PRISON - LATE AFTERNOON

Yadeh is in a corner with his headphones on, writing in his journal. He is interrupted by Reshawn, a close friend and one of the inmates.

                    RESHAWN
          Yadeh.

Yadeh doesn't hear him and continues to write. Reshawn gently shoves him to get his attention.

                    RESHAWN
          Yadeh.

Yadeh turns around and he is a full-grown man with the scar of his father's assault indefinitely marked below his right eye.

He turns off his headphones and is very irritated.

                    YADEH
          What's up?

                    RESHAWN
          They just had call for lights
          out. They givin' niggas solitary
          if they ain't in their cells.
          It's time to head back.

                    YADEH
          You always got my back. You
          ain't even supposed to be here,
          it's my fault.

                    RESHAWN
          That's what homies do.

They gently hit each other's hand and Reshawn helps Yadeh up. They walk back to their cells together.

                    RESHAWN
          When you blow up on the outside,
          I roll with' you?

                         YADEH
          Nigga, you can't rap.

                         RESHAWN
          So, I'll carry speakers or
          keep the hoes in line for you.

Both start laughing. Yadeh grabs him by the neck as
they make their way down the hall.

                         YADEH
              You got it.

They make their way back to Yadeh's cell where he
is introduced to his new cellmate. Before he could
even make it back to his cell there is a crowd of
individuals blocking the way to his cell. Many
inmates are gathering around because it's Tupac
Shakur. The guards break up the crowd and Yadeh is
able to get to his bunk.

Both men stare each other down before greeting.

                         YADEH
              What up?

                         TUPAC
          What's happening?

Tupac begins setting up on the top bunk.

                         YADEH
              That's my spot, homie. You
              gotta set up down low.

                    TUPAC
        No sweat. Don't want any
        problems.

                    YADEH
        Letting you know.

They stare at each other for another minute.

                    YADEH
            Yadeh.

                    TUPAC
            Tupac.

                    YADEH
            Aight.

Lights flash off. Both men jump on their bunks.

                    TUPAC
        Yadeh, what you do? You kinda
        young to be in here, ain't you?

                    YADEH
        (pauses) Wrong place, wrong time.

                    YADEH
            You?

                    TUPAC
            Being me.

EXT. FABULOUS FOX THEATRE - EARLY AFTERNOON

Al Smith

The marquis on the building reads "Tryouts for the
Atlanta Ballet Dance Troupe today and tomorrow."

Jazmyne anxiously looks at the sign and enters
through the front doors.

INT. BACK STAGE OF THE THEATRE

Full of men and women in tights nervously dancing
around to get out their jitters. Jazmyne is one of
them. She sits down to adjust one of her garments
and is joined by another prospective dancer, Katie.
She looks at the shoes Jazmyne has and gets
excited.

                    KATIE
          Capezios?

                    JAZMYNE
          Yes.

                    KATIE
          Good shoes.

                    JAZMYNE
          Thanks.

                    KATIE
          You're new. Never seen you
          before.

                    JAZMYNE
          I'm Jazmyne.

                    KATIE
Katie. (pauses) I've been
around here awhile. I've been
with the ballet for five years.
I don't know why they keep
making us tryout year after
year. What number are you?

                    JAZMYNE
Seven.

                    KATIE
Good number. Don't be worried.
I'm sure that you'll do just fine.
What are you performing?

                    JAZMYNE
Uh, well, I am doing an
improvisation dance type thing.

                    KATIE
Interesting. How's your
demi plié?

                    JAZMYNE
Demi plié? What's that?

Katie gets up and signals for Jazmyne to join
her. She gently guides Jazmyne through the steps.
Jazmyne is very uncomfortable following her
instructions.

                    KATIE
It's simple. All you do is bend
your knees. You want your knees
to go out and above your feet

                    KATIE (Cont'd)
          in line with them. You don't
          have to go all the way down,
          but you want to keep your heels
          together. As you're slowly
          bending, gracefully move the
          arm that is not on the bar up.
          You want to give the illusion
          that you're floating. Extend
          your arm until it is in line
          with your shoulder. You don't
          have to stiffen the arm and
          make it perfectly straight.
          Remember, ballet moves are
          supposed to be graceful and
          fluid. You don't want to look
          like a robot. Then you will
          place your arm back down slowly,
          and stand back up. Trust me,
          add this into your routine
          today and I guarantee that
          they will choose you.

                    JAZMYNE
          Why you helping me?

                    KATIE
          That's what I'm supposed to do.

Jazmyne looks confused, trying to understand the
comment. A man calls back stage for six, seven,
and eight.

                    JAZMYNE
          That's me. Wish me luck.

                    KATIE
          I don't believe in luck.
          I'll pray for you.

                    JAZMYNE
          Right. (looks perplexed)

They give each other a final look and Jazmyne whisks
away to the auditorium.

INT. GEORGIA STATE PRISON - YEARS LATER- DAY

Prison guard walks down a long hallway with
dangling keys. He finally reaches Yadeh's jail cell.
Yadeh is startled by the sound of the keys.

                    GUARD
          It is the moment of truth.
          Let's go.

Yadeh has things packed and proceeds to walk in
front of the prison guards. They stop into another
room to do a final check of his things and he has
notebooks and notebooks of poetry.

The prison guard continues to rattle keys.

                    YADEH
          Yo, why you got so many keys?
          It's been four years and all I
          see you do is open up these two
          doors. Why you have to have so
          many keys?

                    GUARD
        Well, you ain't got to worry
        about that now. Unless you plan
        on coming back. Don't come back.

                    YADEH
        You threatenin' me now? Last
        man I knew carried all them
        keys like you put this scar
        on my face. I promised if I
        ever saw him again, I'd kill
        him. Watch who you threatenin',
        playboy.

One of the guards rambles through Yadeh's
belongings.

                    YADEH
        Yo, I'm leaving. Why ya'll
        gotta search my stuff?

                    GUARD
        Gonna do anything with these?

Guard holds up a notebook.

                    YADEH
        Time will tell.

EXT. GEORGIA STATE PRISON - DAY

Yadeh proceeds to walk outside. He stops and digs
and shuffles through his notebooks and finds what he
is looking for. It's Tupac's contact information.
It reads, "Holler at me when you get out - PAC
(323) 555-1212." He looks up and starts smiling.

INT.STUDIO - NIGHT

Tupac and the engineer are listening to a track
without vocals. The room is filled with weed smoke
and attractive women.

                    TUPAC
          I think we have a banger for
          this one. Moe Bee, you've done
          it again.

Tupac gets up and walks into the sound booth.

                    ENGINEER
          Where do you want to start?

                    TUPAC
          Just hit play and let it ride.
          I gotta feel it again.

The camera shows Tupac's reflection off of the sound
proof glass. There is a knock on the door and one
of the roadies opens the door. It's Yadeh and his
friend Reshawn from jail.

                    ROADIE
          May I help you?

                    YADEH
          Pac around?

                    ROADIE
          He's busy right now. You gotta
          check in later.

                         YADEH
              Don't think so, homie. He told
              me to come holler at him.

                         ROADIE
              Hold on. Who you?

                         YADEH
              Tell'em cell 93452.

Roadie looks at him confused, closes the door
slightly.

                         ROADIE
              Yo, tell Pac some nigga from
              cell 93452.

The music stops in the middle of Tupac's verse.

                         TUPAC
              Why you stop the music? That
              was my best take so far.

                         ENGINEER
              A guy from 93452 said you told
              him to come up here.

                         TUPAC
              93452? Yadeh?

Tupac takes off his headphones and runs out of the
booth. They run and give each other a big hug.

                         TUPAC
              You finally out, huh? You done
              beefed up?

              YADEH

Liftin' and writin'.

              TUPAC

I hope your rhymes is as good
as your liftin'. You on payroll
now. Step into the chamber and
make me my money.

              YADEH

Word?

              TUPAC

Go.

INT. STUDIO SOUND BOOTH

Yadeh walks in the sound booth, adjusts the
headphones. Tupac jumps into the pilot's seat.

              TUPAC

I'm a start it from the
beginning. Wait four bars and
then do what you do.

Tupac hits the button. The beat drops. It rides and
Yadeh stumbles. He's a little nervous. This is a
very awkward moment for him.

              TUPAC

Yadeh, relax. Don't try to kill
it on the first take. Treat the
track like a woman.(starts
laughing) Well, you probably
haven't seen one

> TUPAC (Cont'd)
> of those for a long time.
> Start slow and then go in for
> the kill. I'm a start it from
> the top.

Yadeh begins rapping and begins feeling it and
kills the verse.

MONTAGE:

- Yadeh and Pac at a music conference

- Chart topping single, Tupac featuring Yadeh Ya

- Yadeh back in the studio

- Radio interviews

- Magazine story: Years after Tupac's death, Yadeh
  is hip hop's next hope

- Hip hop's new school artist

INT. FOX THEATRE AUDITORIUM

An empty theater with the exception of four filled
seats, which contain the judges reviewing the
performance.

Jazmyne nervously walks on stage. The judges are
conversing amongst themselves about the previous
performance. They finally settle down because they
see Jazmyne waiting in front of them.

                    KEN
        So, Ms.… Greer, what will you
        grace us with today?

                    JAZMYNE
        Well, I am not the typical
        dancer. Most of my training has
        been at church. Therefore, I
        will dance to "Come Into My
        Tabernacle."

Judges look at one another, with mixed emotions on
their faces. She proceeds to dance and she woos
them with her closing.

After she dances they mumble amongst themselves for
a second. Then Ken and Frank get into an argument.

                    KEN
        Ms. Greer, who taught you the
        demi plié? I'm very curious.

                    JAZMYNE
        A good friend.

                    KEN
        Is she classically trained?

                    JAZMYNE
        I believe so, yes.

                    KEN
        I can tell from your moves you
        are a praise dancer. Your
        technique is a little rough

                        KEN (Cont'd)
        and edgy, don't you think?
        (looking at Frank)

                    FRANK
        Quite edgy.
                        KEN
        Frank and I have this debate
        on classical training vs. raw
        talent. What you have is
        definitely raw. I like raw.
        Your style is phenomenal,
        the best I've seen in years.
        Ms. Greer, welcome to the
        Atlanta Ballet Company.

The judges start clapping. Frank claps his hands
unwillingly.

Scene cuts to a montage of Jazmyne dancing in front
of mass audiences.

EXT. IN FRONT OF PAPA'S HOUSE MAILBOX - YEARS LATER
- DAY

Papa looks at it. He really can't see that well so
he puts on his reading glasses. It is from Jazmyne.

                    JAZMYNE'S V.O.
        Dear Papa, I know it has been
        years since we've spoken and
        I've received all of your phone
         messages. I felt so bad how I
        left things that I couldn't
        face you. You have done so many
        things for me and I felt that

you didn't deserve how I
treated you. I know my mother
treated you and Grandma just
as bad. And plus, I wanted you
to be proud of me. But the
thing is, who could be proud
of a high school dropout? Life
has been pretty good to me over
the years. I've made it in
dancing. I am the premier
dancer at the Atlanta Ballet
Company. I'm so excited. I'm
ready to see you. I want you to
come and visit me in Atlanta.
I have a performance in one week
and I would love it if you would
come. Tell everybody back home
I said hey. Love, Jazzy

EXT. DOWNTOWN CITY STREET - DAY

People are walking by a larger-than-life billboard
of Jazmyne gliding across the sign. Papa looks
down at his notes, looks up at the billboard and
proceeds into the building.

INT. FOX THEATRE AUDITORIUM - DAY

CG - Good Morning Atlanta.
The program has a brief opening with cheesy music.
A reporter is standing waiting on her cue to begin
an interview with Jazmyne.

                    ANCHOR
          We are back, live at the Fox
          Theatre with the premier dancer

                        for tonight's performance,
                        Jazmyne Greer. Hey,Jazmyne.

                              JAZMYNE
                        Hello.
                              ANCHOR
                        You are the premier dancer for
                        the Atlanta Ballet Company.
                        What does that mean to our
                        audience and what will we expect
                        from tonight's performance?

                              JAZMYNE
                        Being the premier dancer means
                        that I am the lead role in
                        majority of the scenes. Just
                        like a movie, you have the star,
                        or lead, and then you have the
                        supporting cast.

Other dancers, including Katie are standing in the
background watching the interview.

                              ANCHOR
                        And tonight's performance?

                              JAZMYNE
                        Lots of movement, lots of
                        dancing, colorful costumes …

                              ANCHOR
                        Speaking of moves, you ready
                        to give us a taste of what to
                        expect this evening?

                        JAZMYNE
        Sure.

Anchor steps to the side, next to a brightly smiling Papa. Jazmyne moves into position and begins
dancing. Her supporting cast soon joins her for the
next three minutes and the performance concludes.

                        ANCHOR
        That was beautiful. Wow! Where
        did you learn how to move like
        that? Where do you get your
        inspiration? Your gift is
        heaven sent.

                        JAZMYNE
        Thank you. (out of breath) No,
        not heaven or God but just…
        just deep within. I love to
        dance, ever since I was a child.
        I dig deep within myself and
        pull out everything I can.

Papa's face turns sad, but then tries to smile
again, faking.

                        ANCHOR
        Alasha Strother, Channel 5 News.

The light on top of the camera turns off.

                        CAMERA MAN
        We're good.

The cameraman takes his camera off of his shoulder
and begins disassembling the equipment.

                    ANCHOR
          Jazmyne, that was awesome.

                    JAZMYNE
          Thank you. Oh, I want you to
          meet my grandpa. Papa, this
          is Alasha.

                    PAPA
          Hi, sweetheart. You really
          know your stuff.

                    ANCHOR
          Thank you. Your granddaughter
          is phenomenal.

                    JAZMYNE
          You are too kind. Oh, by the
          way, I have two tickets pulled
          for you for tonight's show.

                    ANCHOR
          Thank you. Jazmyne, if there's
          anything you need or even want
          to come back to the show, let
          me know. You are always welcome.
          And I mean that.

Alasha hands Jazmyne a business card.

                    JAZMYNE
          That's good to know.

Jazmyne turns and looks at Papa. She smiles at
him and walks over to her friends and the other

dancers. They greet her with excitement and Papa remains stagnant with a smile on his face. After the excitement, she walks over to Papa.

                    JAZMYNE
          What you think?

                    PAPA
          You already know. You always
          give stellar performances.

INT. JAZMYNE'S APARTMENT - TUESDAY MORNING

Papa is half asleep on the couch, reading the Bible and watching television. Jazmyne walks in. Her hair is in a mess. She just woke up and she is still half asleep.

                    PAPA
          Morning.

                    JAZMYNE
          Mmmmm.

She walks in to the kitchen and pours a cup of coffee. The program that Papa is watching gets interesting but he strikes up a conversation anyway.

                    PAPA
          How'd you sleep?

                    JAZMYNE
          Good. I'm still tired. I'm glad
          we have today off. I don't think
          I can move another muscle.

                    PAPA
          Sit down, join me.

Jazmyne sits down on the couch and they share a cup
of coffee. They drink and are silent.

                  JAZMYNE
          I'm glad you're here.

Jazmyne put her coffee down and snuggles under him.

                    PAPA
          I miss all of the loud noise
          and all of your friends at the
          house. Josh says hi.

                  JAZMYNE
          Ahhhh, and then there was Josh.

                    PAPA
          How are you?

                  JAZMYNE
          Happy.

                    PAPA
          Good.

                  JAZMYNE
          I'm doing what I love.

                    PAPA
          That's important. (pauses)
          Jazmyne...

They look eye to eye. Jazmyne knows where the
conversation is going.

> PAPA
> No, please hear me out. I've
> always been proud of you. You
> always have this spirit of
> bouncing back through adversity.
> Just like when your mother left,
> or when your grandma died when
> you were six. You wanted to
> speak at her funeral. So many
> people were shocked. What
> six-year-old wants to speak in
> front of people, let alone at
> their grandma's funeral? You
> are a beautiful, bright young
> lady and yes, I am proud of you.

> JAZMYNE
> Thank you, Papa.

They sit for a second in silence.

> PAPA
> I was meaning to ask you, what
> is your inspiration?

Jazmyne looks confused.

> PAPA
> The reporter asked you what
> inspires you?

                    JAZMYNE
God does.

                    PAPA
Come on. Don't tell me what I
want to hear. That's not what
you told the reporter.

                    JAZMYNE
I know, I know. Papa, I don't
know if I really believe in God.
I'm tired of acting like I do
when I really don't know anymore.

                    PAPA
What do you mean?

                    JAZMYNE
I mean, come on, if there is a
God, why did we struggle all
of those years? Why did God
let my mother choose the
streets over me, or let Grandma
die? And I mean, come on, we
went to Sunday school,
vacation Bible school, choir
practice, Bible study…. We
overloaded on God, but we saw
nothing. NOTHING.

                    PAPA
How can you even say that, my
child? God has been so good
to us. He provided a roof,
food, and clothing. We never
needed nothing. You lived well.

                    JAZMYNE
Why is it that all of the
successful people in the city
who denounce God got Mercedes
Benzes, big houses, and
everything? I've never heard
them once say anything about
God, so why should I? I don't
get it.

                    PAPA
Blessed is the man who does
not seek the counsel of the
wicked, or stand in the path
of sinners.

Jazmyne joins in and completes his sentence.

                    JAZMYNE
I know all of that, but that
never helped me with my
problems. It never helped
with our problems.

                    PAPA
Speak for yourself. That is
how I make it though each day.
My treasures aren't here, they
are waiting for me in heaven.
I have peace, knowing that
God is in control of my life.
What you don't clearly
understand about God could be
the very thing you miss and
desperately need.

                        JAZMYNE
            If that's the case, I'd prefer
            to control my own destiny,
            I mean….

The conversation is cut short because both of their
attention focuses on the occurrences taking place
on the television. Jazmyne grabs the remote and
turns the volume up to hear what is going on.

                    NEWSCASTER V.O.
            Ladies and gentlemen, what you
            are about to witness is a true
            occurrence that just happened
            moments ago in New York City.
            Both towers at the World Trade
            Center have fallen. Apparently
            two commercial airplanes ran
            into both towers, causing them
            to crumble within minutes of
            the crash. Reports say that
            this is a terrorist attack on
            America. It is not clear who
            is behind the operation.
            Please stand by to hear more
            details on this tragic event.

CG: TWO DAYS LATER

INT. FOX THEATRE AUDITORIUM - DAY

Jazmyne walks into the room like business as usual,
and she notices that many dancers aren't there. She
looks a little puzzled. She doesn't understand what
is going on. She walks past several dancers as they
make their way out of the door.

                    JAZMYNE
        Ken, what is going on?

Ken looks extremely sad.

                    KEN
        It's over.

                    JAZMYNE
        Talk to me in English.

                    KEN
        Our tour has been cancelled.

                    JAZMYNE
        What? Why? When did this
        happen? I don't understand.

                    KEN
        9/11, the sponsors pulled out.

                    JAZMYNE
        What does 9/11 got to do with
        our show?

                    KEN
        Our sponsor, US Insurance Co.
        People dying. Policies,
        lawsuits, life coverage.

A montage of a series of unfortunate events shows
Jazmyne being turned down for jobs and interviews.
She auditions in front of panel of judges who shake
their heads "no."

Al Smith

During one of her auditions, she runs across a billboard in the hallway with flyers posted to it. The flyers are for a casting call for video dancers in hip hop videos.

INT. KATIE'S LIVING ROOM - EARLY AFTERNOON

Katie is chilling on the couch watching an old episode of "Friends" and the doorbell rings. She gets up, peeps through the peephole and answers the door.

Jazmyne is standing in the doorway crying with a duffle bag.

> JAZMYNE
> I don't have anywhere else
> to go. (crying)

Katie grabs her, hugs her and grabs Jazmyne's things. She ushers her inside the apartment and closes the door.

INT. KATIE'S LIVING ROOM - EVENING

> JAZMYNE
> I must have applied for every
> job in Atlanta. I didn't… don't
> know what else to do?

> KATIE
> Have you thought about going
> back to Americus?

                    JAZMYNE
        I thought about it, but I just
        can't take myself back there.
        So many bad memories. I feel
        like I've failed if I go back.

                    KATIE
        There's nothing wrong with
        hitting a few tough times.
        That's where testimonies are
        made, during the trials. God
        is testing you right now.

                    JAZMYNE
        If that's the case, I know
        that I've failed then.

                    KATIE
        Alright, girl, help yourself
        to anything in the fridge.
        I'm off to bed. I'll see you in
        the morning, bright and early.

                    JAZMYNE
        Bright and early? Tomorrow's
        Sunday. What we got to do
        bright and early?

Cuts to choir scene.

A multicultural choir is singing a contemporary
gospel song.

<Lively contemporary Christian music>

                    KATIE
          I can't wait for you to hear
          our pastor. He tells it like
          it is. No, he's real good.
          His teachings are about the
          cross and how our lives
          should be a living testimony
          of our walk with Christ.
          He's not talking about
          prosperity, money, and how
          to get rich, but focuses on
          the heart and changing the
          mindset. All good stuff.

                    JAZMYNE
          How do you know if he's for
          real, or out to get your money?

                    KATIE
          That is something you really
          have to pray about and ask God
          to give you a discerning heart.

The minister walks up after the choir has just sung
the last selection. The camera shoot never focuses
on the minister's face.

                 MINISTER SPARKS
          Thank you, choir, for ushering
          in the Holy Spirit this morning.
          Everybody, please stand with me
          and tell God He is welcome in
          this house today. Lord, we thank
          you for all the many things that
          you've done in our lives.

                    MINISTER SPARKS (Cont'd)
          We thank you for keeping us
          when we don't want to be kept.
          Lord, we thank you. Everybody,
          just right where you are, just
          talk to Him right now.

Jazmyne looks around at other people in the
sanctuary. She closes her eyes because she sees
everybody with their eyes closed. She slightly
opens her right eye and she sees people crying with
their hands up. Katie begins whispering to Jazmyne.

                    KATIE
          That's Mrs. Julia. Beautiful
          lady, isn't she? She was a
          prostitute for 20 years before
          the Lord delivered her from
          that lifestyle. Now she runs
          a home for women who are on
          the streets and trying to
          change their life.

Jazmyne continues to look throughout the
congregation.

                    KATIE
          And him, that's Larry. The
          doctors pronounced him dead for
          approximately one hour before
          he opened his eyes and began
          speaking. His grandmother came
          into his hospital room and
          prayed over his body for every
          minute of that hour. And he
          came back to life.

MINISTER SPARKS
The title of today's message
is Knowing God. How many people
know God? Come on. It's not a
trick question. Don't be shy.
Raise your hand if you know God.
We're in church, aren't we?
How many people think that
they know God? What do you
understand about God? Are you
satisfied with your current
understanding about Him? How
many know about eternity? The
only way for eternal life is
through Christ. How many
people know that if you're not
interested in knowing God or
having a personal relationship
with God, you're not interested
in eternal life? Turn to your
Bibles to John 17:1. When you
get there, say "Amen."

The room is filled with paper ruffling. While
everyone is turning to the Book of John, the
minister picks up a water bottle and drinks.
The congregation begins to say "Amen."

MINISTER SPARKS
I don't hear a lot of "Amens."
I'll give a little bit more
time for those new Christians.
(begins laughing)OK, this is
Jesus praying for himself
shortly before he is arrested.
The Word reads, "Father, the

MINISTER SPARKS (Cont'd)
          time has come. Glorify your Son,
          that your Son may glorify you.
          For you granted him authority
          over all people that he might
          give eternal life to all those
          you have given him." It goes
          on to say, "Now this is eternal
          life: that they may know you,
          the only true God, and Jesus
          Christ, whom you have sent.
          I have brought you glory on
          earth by completing the work
          you gave me to do."

Minister Sparks stops reading and pauses.

                   MINISTER SPARKS
          That's deep ya'll. Do you know
          what this text means? Eternal
          life? Whew. Knowing God and
          have a relationship with Him
          will grant you eternal life.
          If we knew God the way
          everybody raised their hands,
          we wouldn't do half of the
          stuff we do. Lord knows I'm
          not proud of the majority of
          my past. But God…

Cut to man still trying to find the scripture.

INT. KATIE'S APARTMENT - LATE AFTERNOON

Al Smith

Katie is lying on the couch watching yet another
episode of "Good Times" half asleep. Jazmyne is
getting herself ready to leave. She is being
very quiet because she doesn't want to answer any
questions on her whereabouts. She picks up the
flier and reads where it is.

                    JAZMYNE
          Studio Central off of Courtland.
          Suite A. I know where that's at.

She gets her things, grabs her keys, and sneaks
out. In the process, she drops the flier unknowingly
by the front door.

EXT. CLUB PARKING LOT - LATE AFTERNOON

Jazmyne is walking up to the building and is
looking for the flier. An attractive female
passes her up.

                    JAZMYNE
          Are you going to the video shoot?

                    NEMISHA
          Yeah.

                    JAZMYNE
          I lost my flyer. Where is it?

                    NEMISHA
          Follow me.

                    JAZMYNE
          I don't even know the artist,
          who is it anyway?

                    NEMISHA
        Yadeh Ya. He's supposedly came
        up with Tupac before he died.

                    JAZMYNE
        I'm Jazzy.

                    NEMISHA
        Nemisha, call me Misha.
        Your first shoot?

                    JAZMYNE
        Yep.

                    NEMISHA
        I can tell. It's easy money.
        I always get on these sets.

The two girls walk into the building and there is a
long line of beautiful girls waiting to be picked.
Breet Phillips, a well-known video director,
approaches them.

                    BREET
        You girls here for the Yadeh
        shoot?

Both girls nod.

                    BREET
        OK, you are the last two.

He passes them and locks the door. He puts a
hand written sign up that reads "Casting call is
closed."

Al Smith

The two girls manage to find a seat.

                    BREET
          Thank all of you for coming,
          but we won't be able to use
          all of you. Please standby and
          Yadeh will come and pick who
          he wants.

INT. KATIE'S APARTMENT - EARLY EVENING

Katie is still on the couch and is awaken by the
telephone. She stumbles and grabs the phone.

                    KATIE
          (clears throat) Hello.

                    JOSH
          May I speak to Jazmyne?

                    KATIE
          Hold on.

Katie gets up, walks around the apartment but
doesn't see her around.

                    KATIE
          She must have left. I didn't
          hear her leave. That's odd.
          She normally tells me when she
          leaves. (pauses) May I take a
          message? Josh? OK. Hey, I've
          heard a lot about you. Does she
          have your number? Hold on and
          let me get a pen.

Katie continues to walk throughout the apartment and sees the flier that Jazmyne dropped on the floor. She picks it up, flips to the back side of the flier, and begins to write.

                    KATIE
          OK, I'm ready. 404? That's an
          Atlanta number. You here? You
          moved here? Oh, Jazz is gonna
          be excited. OK, 404-843- uhm mm.
          Got it. Wow! That's neat.
          I can't wait to meet you.
          Alright. Bye bye.

Katie turns the paper over to see what she's just written on. After she reads about the video shoot she looks troubled.

INT. ONSET OF VIDEO SHOOT - EARLY EVENING

The women at the set are beginning to get anxious. Everyone is waiting to be called.

                    JAZMYNE
          Girl, you are a trip for real.
          A car and your rent?

                    NEMISHA
          I'm tellin' you, these rappers
          are suckas.

                    JAZMYNE
          That's wild! But what do they
          get in return?

Al Smith

The director walks out (slow motion) and Yadeh
follows behind along with his friend Reshawn.

                    BREET
          OK, let's make this fast, we
          are behind schedule.

                    YADEH
          Breet, relax, please. This is
          a delicate process. You act
          like this is the first video
          you've directed. You know the
          process. You gotta get the
          right girls.

                    BREET
          You only need seven.

                    YADEH
          OK, OK. (begins looking around
          and points to girls)You. And
          you. You… and you. Hi!(looks
          at female) You. Her.

Yadeh continues to look around. Nemisha gets up and
walks toward Yadeh.

                    NEMISHA
          Hey, Yadeh.

                    YADEH
          Hey, sweetheart…

                    NEMISHA
          Misha.

                    YADEH
        Right...Misha.

                    BREET
        Lady, please sit down.

                    YADEH
        She's aight. Come on over,
        sweetheart. She's girl seven.

Yadeh's friend points out Jazmyne.

                    RESHAWN
        Yo, Yadeh... You gotta get her.
        She's fine as hell.

Jazmyne blushes.

                    BREET
        We only have room for seven,
        one has to go.

Yadeh pauses for a minute. He turns to Nemisha.

                    YADEH
        Sorry, sweetheart, maybe on
        the next one.

Then Breet opens the door and begins pushing
everyone out who wasn't selected, starting with
Nemisha. Nemisha gives Jazmyne an evil look.

Once he closes the door, the camera follows behind
the girls as they make their way on the set.

                         BREET
          OK, I need all ladies to the
          hair and wardrobe area pronto.
          Ladies and gentlemen, we have
          10 minutes before we start
          production.

Yadeh grabs Jazmyne.

                         YADEH
          Girl seven, what's your name?

                        JAZMYNE
          Jazmyne.

                         YADEH
          Jazmyne, I'm Yadeh.

                        JAZMYNE
          Hi.

                         YADEH
          I look forward to working
          with you.

A young female, the stylist, walks up to Jazmyne.
She looks Jazmyne up and down and holds up five
skimpy outfits. She thumbs through them. She picks
one and hands it to Jazmyne.

                     VIDEO STYLIST
          Here, put this on, then go to
          the hair and makeup station
          right over there. The bathroom
          is off to the right once you
          pass the double doors.

CG: TWENTY MINUTES LATER

Jazmyne walks from the hair dressing station and
she literally stops everyone in their tracks.
Everyone, including Yadeh, stops and stares.

The director is trying to place the girls within
the scene. He attempts to put another girl right by
Yadeh while he's rapping.

                    YADEH
          No, I want girl seven beside
          me on this scene.

Jazmyne is extremely flattered. She walks past the
other girls and they are all envious.

The director walks up to Yadeh.

                    BREET
          Uh, Yadeh. She was the main
          girl in all of the scenes
          since we started.

Reshawn has been eyeing Jazmyne since the set
started.

                    YADEH
          So.

                    BREET
          We aren't selling relationships.
          We are selling sex, lots of sex.

                    YADEH
          Is this your video or mine?

                         BREET
          You're the boss. (frustrated)

Jazmyne blushes. The music begins and he starts
rapping and they connect eyes continuously.

CG: EIGHT HOURS LATER

The crew is tearing down the set and Jazmyne is
leaving. Reshawn runs up to Jazmyne and tries to
spark a conversation.

                         BREET
                 Ladies, please make sure you
                 fill out the time sheets with
                 your contact information so
                 we can pay you.

All of the ladies are filling out the forms then
begin to leave.

                        RESHAWN
                 A, you did your thing on the
                 set today. Congratulations.

                        JAZMYNE
                 Thank you. And thank you for
                 picking me earlier. I really
                 appreciate it.

                        RESHAWN
                 No problem. (pause) I normally
                 don't come off like this but I
                 don't know if I'll ever see
                 you again.

                    RESHAWN {Cont'd)
Do you mind if we exchange
numbers? I'd like to get to
know you.

                    JAZMYNE
I don't think that's a good
idea. Not right now. Sorry.

                    RESHAWN
You sure? Well, here take mine.
Think about it and call me if
you want to.

                    JAZMYNE
OK. Thanks.

She leaves the building and into the parking lot.
She turns around to see if he's looking then balls
up the paper and throws it on the ground. She
smiles because her self-esteem has just received
another push.

INT. CLUB HALLWAY - EARLY EVENING

Reshawn looks from the window. Yadeh walks up.

                    YADEH
        She's a fine one, ain't she?

                    RESHAWN
        You ain't never lied.

With her makeup and hair still done, Jazmyne
decides to go to the mall. She feels pretty and
wants to continue receiving attention.

EXT. STRIP MALL - NIGHT (DOWNTOWN)

Jazmyne begins walking down the street. She gets many looks. She smiles and stops at a window and sees a gorgeous wedding dress.

EXT. FRONT PORCH - NIGHT - FLASHBACK

                    JAZMYNE
          Papa, you think I'll ever get
          married?

                    PAPA
          When the time is right, when
          the time is right.

CUT BACK TO PRESENT - WINDOW SHOPPING SCENE

EXT. STRIP MALL - NIGHT (DOWNTOWN)

Window lights turn off. A sales associate flips the store sign to read "Closed." In the same window, Jazmyne sees a beautiful summer dress. She admires it.

INT. KATIE'S APARTMENT - NIGHT

Katie is on the couch reading. She looks at Jazmyne and continues reading.

                    KATIE
          How was it? The video shoot?

Jazmyne looks surprised.

                        KATIE
         You dropped the flier by the
         front door. Oh, by the way,
         Josh called while you were
         gone. He said call him. The
         number is on the kitchen
         counter. Also, some guy named
         Yadeh called you. His number
         is on there too.

Jazmyne walks to the kitchen counter, picks up
the messages written on the back of the flier,
and proceeds back to her room. She picks up the
cordless phone and dials Josh's number.

                      JAZMYNE
         Shut up! (loudly)Oh my God!
         Oh my God!

Katie gets up and walks to the doorway of Jazmyne's
room and smiles.

                      JAZMYNE
         When did you move here? And
         why you just now calling?
         We have got to hook up. Like
         right now.

INT. RESTAURANT - NIGHT

It is an extremely busy night for the local
restaurant on this Saturday evening. Jazmyne, Josh,
and Katie are sitting at a table.

                    JAZMYNE
    So I'm like, "Josh! Get out of
    there before…" Too late. Here
    comes Mama Shepherd with a
    switch, and she said, "Boy you
    'bout to get the beatin' of
    your life."

Josh joins in.

              JOSHUA AND JAZMYNE
    "Now go on in the house while
    I deal with Mrs. Twiddle Toes."

                    KATIE
    Ya'll really like brother and
    sister, huh?

                    JAZMYNE
    Yeah, that's my ace.

Josh looks saddened, but still is smiling.

                    KATIE
    So where you workin'? What you
    doing?

                    JOSH
    I got a job at the news station
    as a segment producer. I'm
    also going to do freelance
    photography on the side.

                    JAZMYNE
    He loves that camera. He is
    really talented.

                    JOSH
          Matter of fact.

Josh reaches in his bag and pulls out a camera and
hands it to Katie.

                    JOSH
          Can you take a picture of Jazz
          and me?

                    KATIE
          I don't know how to work this
          fancy camera.

                    JOSH
          All you do is point and click.

He gets it back from her, sets the lens and hands
it back to her.

                    JOSH
          There you go.

Josh and Jazmyne scoot their chairs together.

                    KATIE
          Say "cheese."

Katie snaps the picture.

                    KATIE
          So, Josh, you find a church
          home yet?

                    JOSH
          Nope. You got a church for me?

                    KATIE
          You know I do. Come with us
          next time. Tomorrow!

                    JOSH
          I'm there.

Katie hands the camera back to Josh. He looks at
the settings again. He hands it back to Katie.

                    JOSH
          Here, can you take another one?
          I'm not sure the first shot is
          a clear one.

Josh and Jazmyne lean in again and Katie takes the
picture.

                    KATIE
          I'm gonna warn you. I go to
          the 8 a.m. service.

INT. JAZMYNE'S BEDROOM - EARLY MORNING

The alarm clock reads 7:15 a.m. Katie walks in
the room.

                    KATIE
          I take it you're not going
          this morning. Josh is in the
          TV room waiting on you.

Jazmyne rolls around with her eyes shut.

                    JAZMYNE
      Tell him and Jesus I'll catch
      up with them later. I'm tired.

Katie pauses and then closes the door.

INT JAZMYNE'S BEDROOM - LATE MORNING

The clock now reads 11:17 a.m. The phone rings.
Jazmyne shuffles around and picks it up.

                    JAZMYNE
           Hello. (clearing voice)

                    YADEH
      So were you gonna call me back?

                    JAZMYNE
           Who is this?

                    YADEH
      Who is this? We spent all
      day together. All up in each
      other's face and now you
      catch amnesia.

                    JAZMYNE
      Yadeh?

                    YADEH
      What's the deal? Sounds like
      you sleep. You seemed like a
      lil' church girl. I figured I'd
      get your voicemail. You got
      plans today?

Al Smith

Jazmyne perks up while smiling.

INT. RESTAURANT - DAY

Jazmyne is a little timid being with a celebrity.

                    JAZMYNE
          So is this how you treat all
          of your video vixens?

                    YADEH
          Ahhh, no just the ones I like.

                    JAZMYNE
          Oh, the ones you like. So there
          are others?

                    YADEH
          Well….

Two young girls walk up.

                    GIRL ONE
          Excuse me, Mr. Ya. Can we take
          a picture with you?

Yadeh looks up to them and begins smiling.

                    YADEH
          Absolutely.

                    GIRL ONE
          (facing Jazmyne) Do you mind?

The girl hands Jazmyne the camera.

                    JAZMYNE
          Why not?

Jazmyne takes the picture.

                    GIRLS
          Thank you.

                    JAZMYNE
          Do you ever get tired of that?
          Everyone is always looking
          at you.

                    YADEH
          Yeah, sometimes. But they pay
          my rent, my car, this lunch
          you swallowed down in 45
          seconds. (both laugh)

                    JAZMYNE
          Everyone seems to love you.
          Like how on the video set your
          friends just really admire you.

                    YADEH
          I just try to take care of my
          people. I know what it's like
          to not have nothing, or
          anybody to help you out when
          times get hard. Pac gave me
          that chance long time ago.
          He said always take care of
          your people and your fans and
          they will love you for it.

EXT. STRIP MALL - DAY

                    YADEH
My folks threw me out while I
was 14. I didn't graduate. My
father and I never got along.
If I would've stayed, one of
us would be dead.

                  JAZMYNE
Do you talk to them now?

                    YADEH
My mother died a couple of
years ago to breast cancer.
I haven't talked to my father
in years. He has left a couple
of messages for me, but I
never called him back.

                  JAZMYNE
How come you never called
him back?

                    YADEH
I got nothing to say to him.
(becomes uncomfortable)So tell
me about you.

                  JAZMYNE
I never knew my dad. I was told
he was a guitarist for the
Whispers and the Bee Gees. My
mom left when I was five. My
grandfather raised me. My story
is pretty short and simple. I
wanted to do something with my
life, so I moved from a small

JAZMYNE (Cont'd)

town of Americus to here. You
heard of Americus?

YADEH

Yeah, I think… Nah, I ain't
heard of Americus.

JAZMYNE

It's known for having bats.

YADEH

Bats? Most towns are known for
peaches, corn, potatoes, good
restaurants… bats?

JAZMYNE

Yeah, long story. My grandfather
is a butterfly farmer.

YADEH

A butterfly farmer? (starts
laughing) Black folks don't
raise butterflies.

JAZMYNE

My granddaddy does. (becomes
defensive)

YADEH

(laughing) OK, OK. I didn't
mean to make you mad.

Jazmyne's frown turns into a smile. They walk past
the window she was at the previous night.

                    JAZMYNE
        What do you think of the dress?

                    YADEH
        (Yadeh looks at the wedding
        dress.) Uhm, this is the first
        date. I ain't even got the
        panties yet. Why you lookin'
        at wedding dresses? I think
        you're moving too fast!
        (laughing)

                    JAZMYNE
        Oh, you got jokes. You think
        you getting some? (laughing)
        I'm talking about the dress
        next to it.

                    YADEH
        Oh! Yeah, I'm just playing.
        Uhm, yeah I like it. Let's go
        try it on.

                    JAZMYNE
        Nah… I don't feel like it.

                    YADEH
        Come on. Have a little fun.

Jazmyne hesitates.

                    JAZMYNE
        Alright.

They walk into the store.

INT. STORE DRESSING ROOM - DAY

Jazmyne walks out.

> JAZMYNE
> You think?

> YADEH
> That looks good. You are a
> gorgeous…. That's real. Yo,
> try on another one. Excuse me.
> (he gets the attention of the
> sales associate) Can she try
> on some more of these same
> type dresses?

> SALES ASSOCIATE
> Sure. Hold on.

Jazmyne walks out three or four times with
different dresses. Yadeh has all of the dresses
in his hands.

> YADEH
> We'll take all of them. (gives
> to sales associate)

> JAZMYNE
> I can't accept this.

> YADEH
> Why not? Take'em. I don't
> expect nothing in return.
> It's a gift.

He proceeds to the cash register.

                    JAZMYNE
          Thank you.

                     YADEH
          No problem.

Montage of Jazmyne and Yadeh falling for one
another.

- Jazmyne and Yadeh ride in car

- Walk in Centennial Park

- On the set of another video

- Yadeh with Jazmyne on a cover of famous magazine

- TV Entertainment program featuring Jazmyne

- Jazmyne on the cover of King magazine

EXT. DOWNTOWN OUTSIDE BUSINESS BUILDINGS - LATE DAY

Jazmyne and Yadeh are walking into the building and
a reporter stops them. Yadeh is on the phone.

                    REPORTER
          Excuse me, Yadeh?

Yadeh turns around, but continues talking on the
phone.

                    REPORTER
          Hi, I'm Walter Mitchell. I'm
          with Street Grime Magazine.

Reaches out to shake Yadeh's hand.

                    REPORTER
          I would like to get an
          interview with you if you
          don't mind. I would like to
          talk about your latest CD and
          future projects.

                    YADEH
          Hold on…. Who you with?

                    REPORTER
          Street Grime.

                    YADEH
          Can't help you.

Jazmyne looks at the reporter.

                    JAZMYNE
          Sorry, it's just people try
          to get at him all the time.

Jazmyne continues to follow behind Yadeh.

                    REPORTER
          Yeah, I understand.

INT. RADIO STUDIO - DAY

The two are in the studio with Reshawn capturing
the upcoming interview on a video camera.

                    FLEX ONE
          Flex One, coming through the

                    FLEX ONE (Cont'd)
          airwaves, that's Yadeh's latest,
          titled "Dead Man Walking.
          "That joint right there is hot!
          We got Yadeh up in the studio
          with hip hop's hot girl,
          Jazmyne. Peoples, what's up?

                  YADEH AND JAZMYNE
          What's going on?

                    FLEX ONE
          Ya'll like hip hop's Bonnie
          and Clyde!

Everybody laughs.

                    FLEX ONE
          Na for real, Yadeh. Let's talk
          about the album. It's called
          Eulogy. It's a dark album.
          Tell us about it.

                    YADEH
          Yeah… Eulogy. It's about my
          experience growing up in the
          streets. It's so real because
          every cat that's in the
          streets trying to stay alive
          can feel it.

                    FLEX ONE
          "Dead Man Walking, "the first
          single off the album. Talk to
          me about how you came up with
          that? It's a dope song.

                    YADEH
Hate inspired that song.

                    FLEX ONE
Dang, that's deep. Hate?
That's strong.

                    YADEH
It's directed toward an
individual who tried to write
my death sentence. And I'm a
leave it at that.

                    FLEX ONE
Is it another MC? We got
another beef going?

                    YADEH
Nah, nothing like that. But
I'm a leave it there.

                    FLEX ONE
Bonnie—I mean, Jazmyne—
(everybody starts laughing)
tell me about the calendar.

                    JAZMYNE
It comes out in two weeks.
You can find it at any book
store. Basically, the calendar
captures every personality and
mood that I have.

Al Smith

                    FLEX ONE
          (cuts in) Jazmyne, lookin' at
          these, got a lotta personality.
          (everybody laughs)

                    JAZMYNE
          There are some provocative
          pictures and some fun pictures.

                    FLEX ONE
          I see! Yadeh, you's a lucky man!
          Got any sisters?!!!(everybody
          laughs)Yadeh Ya and Jazmyne
          Greer up in the studio. The
          number is 404-triplezero-WTTX,
          call and holler at Yadeh
          or Jazmyne.

Flex One pushes a couple of buttons and music
begins playing. Everybody in the studio is
playing around and having a good time. Jazmyne
and Yadeh start dancing to the music. The music
plays for a short moment, and Flex One pulls the
microphone close to his mouth.

                    FLEX ONE
          Oh, my goodness. The phone
          lines lit up like Christmas
          lights. WTTX, who is this?

                    CALLER ONE
          This is Tre.

                    FLEX ONE
          What's up Tre?

                    CALLER ONE
What's up?

                    FLEX ONE
Who do you want to speak to?

                    CALLER ONE
I got a question for Yadeh.

                    YADEH
What's up Tre?

                    CALLER ONE
Yo, what's up? I used to stay
over there down the street
from your house off MLK.

                    YADEH
Aight, aight.

                    CALLER ONE
I got a couple of tracks that
I want to you to hear. It's
the truth. I'm an MC. How can
I get it to you?

                    YADEH
Well...

                    FLEX ONE
Drop it off or email it to the
studio and I'll see that Yadeh
gets it. WTTX, who's this?

                    CALLER TWO
This is Marcus.

                    FLEX ONE
What's up, Marcus?

                    CALLER TWO
Nothing. I wanted to holler
at Jazmyne...

                    JAZMYNE
Hey, Sweetie...

                    CALLER TWO
Hey, Jazmyne. You's a fine one.

                    JAZMYNE
Well, thank you, Marcus.
That's so sweet.

                    CALLER TWO
I just see you in Yadeh's
videos. Will you ever do any
other rapper's video?

                    YADEH
(cuts in) No. I can answer
that one for her. (everyone
laughs)

                    FLEX ONE
WTTX, who's this?

                    CALLER THREE
Yadeh... Yadeh, you there?
This is your father.

The room becomes silent.

                    YADEH
What?

                 CALLER THREE
How you doin'?

                    YADEH
I'm doin'. What do you want
to say?

                    CALLER
I just called to check on
you and….

                  FLEX ONE
Excuse me, pops, we gotta run
to a commercial break while
the family makes their ties.
We'll be right back.

Commercial begins in the background.

                  FLEX ONE
You can pick the phone up
right outside there in the
lobby.

Yadeh gets up and goes out there. He picks up the
phone and begins yelling. Jazmyne tries to distract
everyone in the studio.

                   JAZMYNE
Soo. How long you been at the
radio station?

Al Smith

Flex One looks back at Yadeh and trying to get an understanding as to what is going on.

                    FLEX ONE
          Seven years.

                    JAZMYNE
          Seven, that's a good number.
          Uhm. Can you change the mood
          of the interview, if you don't
          mind? Have him rap or something.

Then Flex One turns to the intern and gives them a cue. The intern interprets the hand gesture and begins pushing buttons.

                    FLEX ONE
          Go tell Yadeh we need him back
          in, we are about to go back
          on air.

The intern opens the door and the group hears him yelling. The intern is scared to tell him and is very passive.

                    INTERN
          Mr. Ya, it's time to go back in.

Yadeh looks at the intern and nods. He hangs up the phone and walks back into the studio.

                    FLEX ONE
          You aight?

Yadeh is sweating and breathing heavily.

                    YADEH
Yeah…. I'm aight.

                    FLEX ONE
You up to freestylin'?

                    YADEH
Hell yeah, let's do it.

                    FLEX ONE
WTTX, and we're back with
Yadeh Ya and hip hop's video
eye candy, the beautiful
Jazmyne. Yo, before I let you
leave outta here, you gotta
spit at least 16. Every MC
that comes through here gives
me at least 16 bars. This is
a litmus test to weed out the
fakers from the real MCs.
You down?

                    YADEH
Let's do it.

                    FLEX ONE
Go step into the booth. Flex
One, makin' it do what it do.

Flex scratches an instrumental in. Yadeh gets up
and walks up to another microphone.

Yadeh begins free styling. In his freestyle he
talks about his father discretely. In one verse
he says "You's a dead man." Reshawn continues to
videotape the entire session.

                    FLEX ONE
          Oh my goodness. You murdered
          it. That has gotta be the
          dopest 70 bars I've heard in my
          life. I'm not kiddin'. Oh my
          God. WTTX, history was made
          here in the studio today.
          History.

FADES OUT.

INT. YADEH'S PLACE - EARLY EVENING

Jazmyne has the video camera walking through his
place being the narrator.

                    JAZMYNE
          History, he said. History was
          made today. How do you feel?

                    YADEH
          Good.

                    JAZMYNE
          You sittin' on top of the
          world right now.

                    YADEH
          I'm tryin' to take over the
          world.

                    JAZMYNE
          So what's next for the ruler?

> YADEH
>
> I want to start by takin' over
> the video camera.

They both laugh. The camera shakes when they exchange the camera.

> YADEH
>
> My dime piece.

Jazmyne smiles.

> YADEH
>
> Dance for the camera.

Jazmyne starts doing the Running Man. They both laugh.

> YADEH
>
> I'm serious. Dance for me like
> you do in my videos.

The camera shifts to the stereo system, which shows Yadeh's hand turning it on and some weird techno, exotic music comes on. Jazmyne begins dancing.

Yadeh puts the camera on a tripod and walks into the picture and they begin kissing. They also begin taking their clothes off. The lights go off but the light on the video camera remains on.

FADE TO BLACK.

BLACK AND WHITE IMAGE

Jazmyne is walking down a grassy plain with others dressed in all white gowns. At the bottom of the hill is a country creek. A preacher in a white robe is waiting for all of these people in the water. He baptizes all of them. One woman in particular begins crying with her hands in the sky toward heaven.

Yadeh abruptly wakes up in a cold sweat. His sudden movement wakes Jazmyne up.

                    JAZMYNE
          You OK?

                    YADEH
          Yeah, I'm aight.

Jazmyne rubs his back, and he shrugs her off of him. He looks at her with an evil look and then lays back down.

                    JAZMYNE
          What was that look about? Did
          I whup your ass in your dream?
          Don't mess with me. I'll do it
          in real life!

Both laugh then begin play fighting. Jazmyne looks at the time and gets up.

                    JAZMYNE
          I'm late. I promised Josh that
          I'd ride with him back home.
          I gotta go. Did you want to go?

                    YADEH
    I'm good. Thanks but no thanks.

                    JAZMYNE
    What you plan on doing for
    Thanksgiving?

                    YADEH
    I'm a lay low and write.

                    JAZMYNE
    You sure you don't want
    to come?

                    YADEH
    I'm sure.

                    JAZMYNE
    Alright, but this doesn't let
    you get away from meeting my
    grandfather. Oh, can I take
    one of your cars?

                    YADEH
    Take the Caddy.

She walks up to him and kisses him.

                    JAZMYNE
    Thanks, baby. See you when I
    get back.

INT. YADEH'S CAR - NIGHT

Al Smith

Josh and Jazmyne are riding back to Americus for an extravagant family dinner/gathering. It's been years since Jazmyne has been back home, and many people are anxious to see her now (as a celebrity).

                    JOSH
          I could've drove my car.

                    JAZMYNE
          You've done so much for me
          throughout my life. I wanted to
          do something nice for you for
          a change.

                    JOSH
          This is a nice car. So tell me
          about the infamous Yadeh.

                    JAZMYNE
          What you want to know?

                    JOSH
          What's he like?

                    JAZMYNE
          I know that he raps about guns
          and violence but he is a sweet
          teddy bear underneath?

                    JOSH
          Yeah? You think I could take
          some pictures at the next
          video shoot?

                    JAZMYNE
        No question. I got you.

Jazmyne holds her fist out and Josh puts his fist up
to hers.

                    JOSH
        So… does he love you?

                    JAZMYNE
        Of course he does.

                    JOSH
        Has he said it?

                    JAZMYNE
        Well, not exactly, but I know
        he does by his actions. Hell,
        he wouldn't let me take his
        car if he didn't.

                    JOSH
        I worry about you.

                    JAZMYNE
        Don't.

                    JOSH
        I can't help it. I just care
        about you so much.

                    JAZMYNE
        Oh that is so sweet. I'm fine.
        I've finally got my life back
        on track.

Al Smith

                    JOSH
How do you gauge that? Success?

                    JAZMYNE
I got money again. I'm happy.
I'm makin' big moves.

                    JOSH
Hmm… I don't know any other
way to say this. Jazmyne,
I love you.

                    JAZMYNE
I love you too!

                    JOSH
No, Hear me. I love you like…
love you. I've been in love
with you since Mrs. Bernstein's
class in the 3rd grade. I
can't shake it. I know in my
heart that I'm supposed to be
with you.

                    JAZMYNE
Josh, we've been through this.
You've always been like a
brother to me. I don't know
what to say? I love you like
a brother. Please don't be mad.
But I don't think we're
supposed to be involved like
that. Plus I'm with Yadeh.

                    JOSH
          Well, I've got it off my chest.
          I'm hurt but I feel better now
          that I've at least told you.

                    JAZMYNE
          You are so silly. Do remember
          this, I'll always be there
          for you.

An old school song comes on the radio. Jazmyne
turns the radio up.

                    JAZMYNE
          Ohhhh, that's my jam. What you
          know about this?

Both begin rapping along with the radio. This
lightens the mood and they begin laughing.

EXT. PAPA'S HOUSE - THANKSGIVING DAY

It's a festive occasion. Children are running in
and out of the house. The older kids are sitting
in the living room watching reality television.
They are really entertained by what's going on.
Not too much conversation is happening but a
lot of laughter. They only talk when there are
commercials. Papa occasionally passes by, he
continuously entertains his guests by offering
them popcorn or something to drink. He goes outside
to play with the younger kids. They are playing
kick ball. He gets tired and comes back into the
house to chill out with the rest of the older kids
and young adults. They talk about celebrities and
how Jazmyne is "in the know."

Al Smith

Suddenly, an entertainment report comes on and it discusses celebrity couples, which grabs everyone's attention. The chatter in the room doesn't completely stop until Jazmyne's picture comes on the screen.

                            VJ
Rapper Yadeh Ya and video vixen Jazmyne Greer make their strut on the red carpet Tuesday night at the MTV Video Music Awards. He wears a pinstripe Christian Frucas and she has to have been the most beautiful woman to grace the red carpet that night. Many of you may not know, but Jazmyne Greer made her debut in Yadeh's "Death Trap" video not too long ago, and recently she has been praised and criticized for her controversial videos with Yadeh. Insiders report that there has been an estimated 9 million downloads of a, let's say, a "not-so-clean version" of the "Death Trap" video and there are talks of a sequel.

                        WOMAN VJ
On a not-so-positive note on Jazmyne: protests and more protests. The video vixen has received a lot of paparazzi attention, but also a lot of news coverage about the protests of her being a bad role model for young women.

Cuts to the protests in Downtown Atlanta.

                      WOMAN VJ V.O.
Not only has Jazmyne been receiving attention from the millions of men in American, she's been ridiculed by many, such as these protestors.

Cuts to random interviews on location of a protest.

                    OLDER WHITE WOMAN
          I'm appalled that this type of
          nonsense is accepted in this
          day and time. Just years ago,
          women were fighting for equality,
          now this. This is setting women
          back years. Years. I really
          hate this and wish that things
          would change.

                    NEWS ANCHOR
          Do you think that they will?

                    OLDER WHITE WOMAN
          Well, that's why we are out
          here today. To make that
          change. Yes.

Cuts to another interview.

                    YOUNG INDIAN WOMAN
          Where I'm from, women are
          treasured and adored by the
          media. Images like this would
          never exist. One thing that I
          am afraid of is my home country
          trying to emulate the United
          States in ways like this.
          This is a calamity here and
          if this comes to India, it
          would be detrimental.

Cuts back to Woman VJ.

Al Smith

                    WOMAN VJ
        Those people were really heated
        up. I hope Jazmyne knows what
        she's doing.(Looking at man VJ)
        Do you have any of her videos?

                       VJ
        Well, let's just say the value
        of my personal video collection
        will be raised when I've
        downloaded that video.

Both laugh.

                    WOMAN VJ
        You are a mess. I need to
        talk to your mama. For more
        in the know, go to
        www.intheindustry.com. I'm
        Arion Phillips.

                       VJ
        And I'm Lance Edwards. Stay
        tuned for the up-to-date
        industry news in the next hour.

The room becomes silent. Papa doesn't make eye
contact with Jazmyne. Everyone is still silent and
feels uncomfortable. Papa gets up and walks out of
the room to his bedroom. Jazmyne looks around for
responses.

Mrs. Shepherd walks in the room.

> MRS. SHEPHERD
> Foods ready. (looks around)
> Why is everyone so quiet?
> Come on, let's eat. Where is
> Johnny?

> RELATIVE ONE
> Back in his room.

> MRS. SHEPHERD
> Well, come on, ya'll, let's eat.
> (yells) Johnny, food is ready.

Everyone goes into the kitchen and lines up to eat.
Several people begin fixing their plates.

> MRS. SHEPHERD
> I know that ya'll ain't eating.
> Johnny has to bless the food.
> Johnny, come on now. Valerie,
> go get Papa.

Valerie leaves the room.

> MRS. SHEPHERD
> OK, what's going on? Why all
> ya'll so quiet?

Jazmyne looks away avoiding eye contact.

> RELATIVE ONE
> Nothing, we were just watching
> TV, that's all.

                         MRS. SHEPHERD
          Ya'll up to something. I ain't
          never heard…

A faint scream comes from the back room and
everybody runs to the back.

Papa is laid across the bed with his eyes open.
He's not breathing. Valerie is trying to talk but
her cry continues.

                         MRS. SHEPHERD
          What happened?

                         VALERIE
          I don't know, he was….
          (gibbering)

                         RELATIVE TWO
          Call 911.

The room is overwhelmed with pandemonium. People
begin crying over Papa.

Fades to black.

INT. HOSPITAL WAITING AREA - NIGHT

Jazmyne is at the lounge area fixing a cup of coffee
and the nurse grabs her attention.

                         NURSE
          Ms. Greer?

                         JAZMYNE
          Yes.

                    NURSE
          The doctor would like to speak
          to you a moment.

Jazmyne follows the nurse back to Papa's hospital
room. The doctor is waiting for her at the door.

                    DR. STEVENS
          Hi. Ms. Greer?

                    JAZMYNE
          Yes.

                    DR. STEVENS
          We have re-run the tests, and
          they still came back the same.
          Your grandfather has a lot of
          internal bleeding around his
          heart, making it extremely
          difficult for the heart to work.
          We can go in and operate, but
          just with his age, we are
          certain that he can't
          withstand the operation.
          I'm sorry.

                    JAZMYNE
          What are you telling me?

                    DR. STEVENS
          Your grandfather is dying.

                    JAZMYNE
          Dying? How soon?

                    DR. STEVENS

                Days… hours….

Jazmyne looks around and begins pacing, then the
tears come. The doctor stands there for a minute
and then is paged on the intercom. The nurse
stands there and consoles her. Jazmyne regains
her composure and walks into Papa's hospital room.

                    JAZMYNE
            (whispering) Papa…. Papa….

Papa turns around and looks at her and smiles.

                    PAPA
            My beautiful butterfly.

She leans over and kisses him on his forehead.

                    JAZMYNE
            Are you in any pain?

                    PAPA
            I have clean drawls on.

                    JAZMYNE
            I'm sure you do, Papa.
            (nervously laughing)

                    PAPA
            Sit with me. I heard the
            doctor. He told me earlier
            that I didn't have too
            much longer.

> JAZMYNE

Scared?

> PAPA

Scared? No. Excited? Yes!

> JAZMYNE

Only my Papa…

> PAPA

Death isn't something you should fear. If you live, you die. I know that there is a better place. Free of sickness and disease.

Jazmyne begins whimpering.

> PAPA

Don't cry for me. Be happy.

> JAZMYNE

You're the only family I got.

> PAPA

Natural family, yes. Don't worry, you'll be taken care of.

A long moment of silence passes. They begin watching television, a sleazy talk show is on.

> JAZMYNE

Is there something that you would like to watch?

                    PAPA
        Do me a favor? Turn off the
        television. Read me a story.

                    JAZMYNE
        What do you want me to read?

Papa points to his bag. She begins looking though
it and sees only the Bible.

                    JAZMYNE
        Papa, I don't know if we have
        enough time for me to read this
        whole book. (laughing)

                    PAPA
        Silly. Just a couple of pages.
        Start at Luke 15:11.

Jazmyne begins thumbing though the book looking
for Luke.

                    PAPA
        I am not proud of all the
        decisions you have made in your
        life and I have forgiven you
        for the pain you have caused,
        but I am so happy to have
        shared my life with you. You
        have been such a blessing to me.
        Let this moment stay with you
        the rest of your days. When
        others cause you sorrow,
        forgive them. You'll be at
        peace. My heart has ripened,
        my joy is warm from the rays

PAPA (Cont'd)
of sunlight that you've casted
on me, my child. I love you.

Jazmyne holds back her tears and finds where the
story begins.

JAZMYNE
"There was a man who had two
sons. The younger one said to
his father, 'Father, give me
my share of the estate.' So he
divided his property between
them. Not long after that, the
younger son got together all
he had, set off for a distant
country and there squandered
his wealth in wild living."

Jazmyne looks up and Papa doesn't move. She
continues reading.

JAZMYNE
"After he had spent everything,
there was a severe famine in
that whole country, and he
began to be in need. So he
went and hired himself out to
a citizen of that country, who
sent him to his fields to feed
pigs. He longed to fill his
stomach with the pods that the
pigs were eating, but no one
gave him anything."

Fades to black.

Al Smith

EXT. BURIAL GROUNDS - DAY - PAPA'S FUNERAL

The scene is black and there is silence. Slowly
the blackness fades into a similar depiction of
Ellis Wilson's painting of "The Funeral."There is a
long line of people waiting to get into the church,
to give their last respects to Papa. He is such a
loved man and the turnout has been phenomenal.

<Music> Soft Strings

INT. CHURCH - DAY

Jazmyne is sitting with Yadeh in the first row of
pews in the church. He is not consoling her at all.
Yadeh gets up and walks off to a corner to watch
her from afar. It's obvious that he doesn't want
to be there. Jazmyne is overwhelmed by sadness.
She tries hard to hold back her tears. There are
moments where she keeps her composure, but
immediately loses it shortly after.

The scene cuts to random people making short
speeches about Papa. The recurring theme is that
he loved the Lord with all of his heart. These
messages are intended for Jazmyne, but she can't
focus on what is being said because of her weeping.

Finally, not being able to take the sadness
anymore, she gets up and leaves. Mrs. Shepherd,
Josh's mother, follows her out.

INT. CHURCH FOYER - DAY

<Gospel Music>

Jazmyne begins pacing around crying. Mrs. Shepherd comes out and tries to console her.

                    JAZMYNE
          I can't do it... I can't do it.

                    MRS. SHEPHERD
          Come here.

She continues to move around.

                    MRS. SHEPHERD
          It will be alright.

                    JAZMYNE
          No, it won't. I get tired of
          hearing this... What am I gon' do?

Mrs. Shepherd just sits and listens.

                    JAZMYNE
          What I'm gon' do?

She begins crying again.

                    JAZMYNE
          What I'm gon' do? He's the
          only family I got.

She continues to cry. She runs to Mrs. Shepherd for consoling.

                    MRS. SHEPHERD
          My child. My child.

                    JAZMYNE
          What I'm gon' do? (crying)

                 MRS. SHEPHERD
          You have always been a fighter.
          You will be just fine. God will
          give you the strength.

                    JAZMYNE
          (crying) God? Why did God take
          him from me?

                 MRS. SHEPHERD
          (holding Jazmyne) Child no one
          lives on this earth forever.
          It was his time to go. He was
          ready. If anybody was ready to
          leave this place, it was your
          granddaddy. He told me to look
          after you.

They just sit there in the foyer for moments more.
People are passing them, on their way inside the
sanctuary to view the body. Many are speaking to
Mrs. Shepherd as they pass by.

Jazmyne stops crying and regains her composure.
Mrs. Shepherd takes a handkerchief and wipes
Jazmyne's eyes.

                 MRS. SHEPHERD
          Ready?

Jazmyne nods her head and they get up. They hold
hands and Mrs. Shepherd escorts her back into the
sanctuary.

Josh is up and he gives his testimony.

                    JOSH
          There is so much to be said
          about Mr. Johnny. He was a
          different type of guy.
          Different is an understatement.
          Who else you know that has a
          big bug sanctuary in their
          front yard? (crowd chuckles)
          It just won't be the same
          driving by his house on 10th
          Street and not seeing him
          inside that big glass dome.
          When I was growing up, I
          thought that thing was from
          outta space.(laughs) One thing
          that I can say is regardless
          of what he was doing, he always
          had time for me. He would
          always say, "Son, there are
          three things that you should
          always do in life. Pay your
          taxes, wear clean drawls every
          day, cause ya never know when
          you might have to go to the
          hospital, and always put God
          first in everything you do."
          Mr. Johnny, I've lived by
          those principles every day of
          my life. Every time that I
          would go past his house, I
          could always hear him singing.
          He was a blessed man, but
          singin' wasn't one of them.
          (crowd chuckles) But he would

                    JOSH (Cont'd)
          always say that the word says
          make a joyful noise. (laughs)
          Every now and again I would
          hear him singing "Goin' Up
          Yonder." He told me that he
          wanted a celebration when he
          left this earth.

Music begins playing.

                    JOSH
          Don't be sad, I know he isn't.
          I know that he is chillin',
          free of pain and the stresses
          of this life.

Josh begins singing.

EXT. GRAVE SITE - THE BURIAL - DAY

<Music "Goin' Up Yonder">

INT. CHURCH BASEMENT - DAY

There is a long line to eat. The elder ladies of
the church have prepared a feast for the family
that includes macaroni and cheese, fried chicken,
cole slaw, green beans, and a host of soul food
desserts. Everyone stares at Yadeh and Jazmyne
because they are stars. Several walk up to say
hello.

Jazmyne brings Yadeh to meet Josh.

                    JAZMYNE
          Hey, Josh, this is Yadeh;
          Yadeh, Josh.

They shake hands.

                    JOSH
          So what are you going to do
          with the farm?

                    JAZMYNE
          Don't know. Those butterflies
          are like his babies. I'd hate
          to sell it. I don't know yet.
          Too many things are happening
          at once. I gotta think.

                    JOSH
          Whatever you need, you know
          that I am here, right?

Yadeh stares at Josh with a smirk, but doesn't say
anything.

                    JAZMYNE
          I know. Thank you.

Yadeh looks uncomfortable with how the
conversation is going so he goes outside
for a bit of fresh air.

INT: PRODUCTION STUDIO (YADEH'S VIDEO SHOOT)- DAYS
LATER

Jazmyne managed to get Josh a photography gig on the video shoot. He was hired to take pictures on the set, and Jazmyne, of course, is there dancing for Yadeh. It is mid way through the shoot and Yadeh is not pleased with how things are going. He is high. He and the rest of his crew have been smoking all day, so they are pretty much out of it.

One of the crew members, Reshawn, has been trying to holler at Jazmyne all day. She is becoming somewhat annoyed by it. Yadeh sees what's going on but really doesn't care. He ignores it because he has moved on to the next video vixen, Nemisha, the "new thing." And plus, Nemisha is willing to be a little bit more promiscuous on the video than Jazmyne. Jazmyne and Nemisha trade stares. Nemisha's opportunity has come to gain all of the attention.

                    YADEH
          Cut! (frustrated) Man, I ain't
          feelin' this today.

                    BREET
          What do you mean?

                    YADEH
          Man... (hesitatingly) I ain't
          feelin' this... The shots... the
          angles... this glittery shit....
          Man, roll playback. I got to
          see what you tryin' to do.
          I'm not seeing the vision.

Yadeh and Breet go back in the background and begin looking at the footage. Yadeh's buddies are in the background plotting. They walk around to Yadeh. Unrecognizable background dialogue begins.

                    YADEH
          Man, what do you want?

Airy noises and sound effects.

Reshawn begins talking but you can't hear what's taking place. Yadeh's buddy never turns to look at Jazmyne, but Yadeh does for a brief second.

EXT. CREEK SCENE - FLASHBACK

Jazmyne is walking into a country creek where she is met with a pastor in an all white robes. She proceeds to get baptized in the water.

INT. YADEH'S BEDROOM - NIGHT

Yadeh abruptly wakes up.

INT: PRODUCTION STUDIO (YADEH'S VIDEO SHOOT) - DAY

Yadeh throws his hands in the air with a gesture saying that he doesn't care. (all in slow motion) Conversation begins to get louder amongst different circles. The camera is still on Yadeh while he disputes with Breet, the director, on the creative direction of the video. The conversation is cut short and Yadeh walks over to Jazmyne and begins talking to her. No one can understand what he is saying, but by how Jazmyne is responding, she becomes hurt, disappointed, and holds in her tears.

Josh is witnessing all of this; however, he just sits to the side and begins rotating his camera lens back and forth.

Jazmyne slowly walks to the dressing room and looks around to see if anyone will notice her absence. Reshawn sees her and proceeds to walk in front of her (about 25 feet). Both approach the dressing room. He has a smirk on his face as he whispers something to one of his boys. You can read his lips. He holds up a hand gesture which says "10 minutes," and gives his friends a pound on the hand. They begin laughing and they watch her as she enters the room passing them. By this time, Reshawn has already entered the room.

Josh is observing the entire thing, but still does not react. He begins sweating. He looks around, and the room is spinning.

EXT. CHURCH - DAY - FLASHBACK

<An airy piano starts playing "Jesus Loves Me">

Jazmyne is singing at church with other little children her age.

INT. PRODUCTION STUDIO (YADEH'S VIDEO SHOOT) BACK DRESSING ROOM - DAY

Reshawn comes in and closes the door behind him. He doesn't close it all the way, which leaves a crack for anyone to come in behind him.

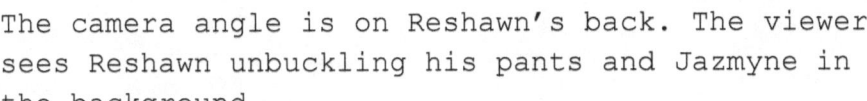

The camera angle is on Reshawn's back. The viewer sees Reshawn unbuckling his pants and Jazmyne in the background.

INT: PRODUCTION STUDIO (YADEH'S VIDEO SHOOT)

Josh is sweating a little bit more and witnesses one of the four guys walking toward the same dressing room. They are giving each other a pound on the hand. Josh is witnessing how the tone of the video shoot has changed. Yadeh begins smoking a blunt and acting foolishly in front of the camera.

<Airy piano continues playing>

> BREET
> Where is Jazmyne? I'm ready to
> get started.

> YADEH
> She's a little preoccupied at
> the moment. (laughing) A… we
> don't need her no way. Just
> roll the damn tape. I say when
> we tape.(pauses for a moment)
> Roll 'em.

His whole entourage starts laughing. The music comes back on.

A few moments later, Reshawn is seen leaving out of the back room putting his clothes back on and another one of Yadeh's entourage leaves to go to the dressing room. Josh hears faint screaming in the background. He continues to turn his lens.

                    RESHAWN
          You heard me beat it out, kid?
          (laughing and playing with
          the others)

CU of Josh's eyes.

CU of Josh turning his lens.

CU of sweat rolling down Josh's forehead.

Random shots of Yadeh's entourage laughing.

Jazmyne can faintly be seen in the back room.
It appears she may be half naked, lying in a
compromising position.

Josh can't take it anymore, as he continues to hear
Jazmyne screaming. He begins moving toward the
dressing room, but gets stopped by the entourage.

                    BUDDY THREE
          Man, I don't think you want
          to go back there right now.
          You might see some things you
          ain't never saw before.
          (laughing)

                    JOSH
          Move.

Josh pushes his way through to the front
doorway of the dressing room. He sees two men
on top of Jazmyne. He hears her screaming. The
entourage jumps on him and starts beating him up.

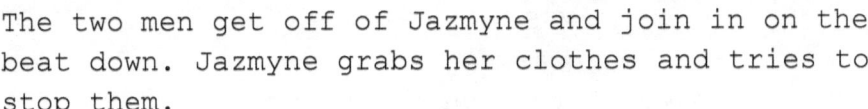

The two men get off of Jazmyne and join in on the beat down. Jazmyne grabs her clothes and tries to stop them.

                    JAZMYNE
              Stop it! You are going to
              kill him!

She tries to help but is unsuccessful. All you can see is blood and the cracked lens of the camera on the floor next to him.

INT. HOSPITAL HALLWAY - LATE NIGHT

Jazmyne runs through the hospital looking for Josh's room in the ER. There is a line standing out of his room with solemn faces.

Josh's sister Sheila notices Jazmyne approaching Josh's room and proceeds to attack her.

                    SHEILA
              You whore! You whore!

People are restraining Sheila.

                    SHEILA
              You whore! My brother almost
              died for you… you slut!

Jazmyne begins to cry. She turns around to leave. Alerted by all of the commotion in the hallway, Mrs. Shepherd comes out and stops her from leaving.

                    MRS. SHEPHERD
He's been asking about you.
He won't rest until he knows
that you are alright. Please
come. As much as I want to
hate you right now, I can't.
You are like a daughter to me.

                    JAZMYNE
Mrs…. I want…

                    MRS. SHEPHERD
Shhhhhhh… I know.

                    JAZMYNE
No, I, I…

                    MRS. SHEPHERD
I know what really happened.
Breet, the director came up
here earlier and told us. Josh
doesn't know that. I know that
you need to get your life
right. Everyone that tries to
love you is willing to die for
you. Who are you willing to
die for?(pause) What are you
willing to die for? Your
behavior triggered Papa's
death. And now maybe my son.
If I told Josh the truth right
now, I know he couldn't take
it. So go in there and tell
him that you love him. Wipe
your tears.

INT. JOSH'S HOSPITAL ROOM - NIGHT

Both women walk in the room and up to Josh's bed.
Josh is brutally beaten.

                    MRS. SHEPHERD
            Josh? Josh, someone came to
            see about you.

Josh slowly responds. He opens his eyes and
slowly smiles. There is a tube connected to his
mouth, which prevents him from speaking.
Mrs. Shepherd looks at Jazmyne, gives her a
half smile, and leaves.

There is a long period of silence.

Jazmyne begins to cry again (silently)

                    JAZMYNE
        I'm....

Josh looks confused.

                    JAZMYNE
        I'm sorry. (begins to cry
        uncontrollably)

Josh begins to tear as well. He reaches for
the camera that is sitting on the nightstand.
He struggles to get it and Jazmyne helps him.

                    JAZMYNE
            What? Your camera?

Al Smith

He nods his head "yes."She's crying still, but
helps him. He barely can hold the camera. His hand
shakes. The camera reaches his face and he manages
to get Jazmyne in the frame of the camera and
begins snapping pictures.

                    JAZMYNE
          I can't believe that you are
          taking pictures. For God's sake,
          you're in the hospital.

He finishes taking pictures and puts it on his lap.

                    JAZMYNE
          Sorry.

Josh reaches his hand to remove the tube so he can
speak. Jazmyne manages to control her weeping, once
more and attempts to stop him from removing the
tube. Finally, she helps him take the tube out.

                    JOSH
          You OK?

Jazmyne nods.

                    JAZMYNE
          I'm worried about you!

                    JOSH
          Don't be, (with emphasis) I
          will be alright. Did you file
          a rape charge? (pauses) I have
          clean drawls on.

Josh begins laughing. The laugh immediately turns into a cough. The family and the medical staff come in and wheel him out. Jazmyne gets shuffled to the back of the crowd. She begins to exit through the hallways. Her tears continue, which turn in to a wail. During this moment, it's like she is alone in a crowded hallway. She's crying, but no one stops to see about her. She begins talking but no one can understand or cares what she is saying. Her wail continues as she exits the hospital. She gets to the parking lot and reaches her car, but can't make it in. She cries out in the parking.

                    JAZMYNE
          I can't take this life anymore.
          I can't take this life anymore.
          Lord, where are you? Where are
          you? I can't see you. I can't
          see you. How can you help me?
          Where are you? I need you in
          my life! I need you, Lord. I
          can't live this life anymore.

INT. PAPA'S HOUSE - LATE AFTERNOON - DAYS LATER

Jazmyne is walking through the house. It's full of cobwebs. Old memories come back to mind. She hears her grandfather's voice. Her sadness causes her to fall to the floor. She misses her grandfather so much. Continuing through the house, she goes to her old room. Her room never changed. There still old pictures of LL Cool J, Right On Magazine articles, and old photos of her in the newspaper. She begins going through drawers and looks at old clothes.

                    JAZMYNE
          What was I thinkin'?(laughs)

She continues rummaging through her stuff and
makes her way to her closet. Once she opens the
closet door, clothes fall out, all over the floor.
Old skates and other miscellaneous things hit her.
A jar is the last item to fall out. It rolls and
spins around. It ends up stopping about 8 feet
away from her. She remembers it quite well.
Hesitant to pick it up, she walks toward it slowly.
She reluctantly picks it up and notices that the
butterfly is still in there. She also notices that
there is a label on it. She doesn't recall putting
a label on it. It has "saved" written on it. She
notices a little movement from the butterfly. She
continues to stare and then she realizes that the
butterfly is still alive after all of these years.
She's freaked out about it and drops the jar. The
butterfly glows and she hesitantly picks it up once
again. Jazmyne is in disbelief of the longevity
of life of the butterfly and brings it closer
to her face. The butterfly begins moving with an
enormous amount of energy. She takes the jar
outside and slowly opens the lid. The butterfly flies
to the rim of the jar and gracefully glides into
the midnight sky. Jazmyne smiles as she follows
its flight. Jazmyne has released all control of
her destiny.

INT. KATIE'S APARTMENT - EARLY EVENING

Katie opens the door and Jazmyne is standing there
looking at her with puppy dog eyes. Katie looks
disgusted and sad at the same time.

                    KATIE
I'm sorry to hear about the
loss of your grandfather.

                    JAZMYNE
I gotta talk to you. Please.
I finally understand what you
were trying to explain to me
earlier. I finally get it.
I'm saved.

                    KATIE

Don't play.

                    JAZMYNE
I couldn't be more serious.
Hear me out.

Katie is trying to close the door on her, but stops
to listen.

                    JAZMYNE
The money, the fame, the
clothes and cars… I don't
live for that anymore. Papa
tried to explain to me what
salvation was but I wasn't
trying to hear him at first.
But, I listened Katie. I
listened. I've prayed. I've
talked to God—we've finally
talked. I finally feel free.

Katie is looking at Jazmyne through the doorway.
She begins tearing up and then they hug. She ushers
Jazmyne into the apartment and closes the door.

INT. KATIE'S KITCHEN - EVENING

Katie and Jazmyne sit at the kitchen table. They
share a cup of tea and cookies.

                    KATIE
          So what you gonna do different?

                    JAZMYNE
          Everything!

Katie looks at Jazmyne.

                    JAZMYNE
          I don't know. I'm going to
          have to take it one day at
          a time.

                    KATIE
          It's a whole lifestyle change.
          And you shouldn't make the
          change because you think it's
          the right thing to do. You
          should make the change because
          your heart is after God. The
          people you associate with…your
          conversation… the places you
          frequent…the things you expose
          your mind and body to….
          (Jazmyne shifts her body in
          the seat.)The biggest thing
          is having a meaningful

                    KATIE (Cont'd)
relationship with God. Praying,
talking with Him, reading
His Word, and my favorite is
ministry.

            JAZMYNE
Whoa, whoa, I don't think I'm
supposed to be preaching and
all that.

                KATIE
Ministry is different than
preaching. You hear the
preacher on Sunday morning,
ministry is a part of your
life that you are showing
others in the world.

            JAZMYNE
Hmmm. It's a lot to think
about.

                KATIE
This is serious! Have you
talked to Josh about the
new you?

            JAZMYNE
No. Kinda scared to talk
to him.

                KATIE
Because?

                    JAZMYNE
He was so messed up when I first
saw him at the hospital. And
plus his family hates me.

                    KATIE
Messed up? What happened?

                    JAZMYNE
Because Josh thinks I was
raped. It's a long story… A
couple of things went down on
a video shoot. I was doing
things that I had no business
doing. Yadeh had me do things…
Josh was there and witnessed
something. He got involved to
protect me. He was beat up… he
is in the hospital. He's been
there for some time now.
Bottom line, his family knows
the truth.

                    KATIE
Jazmyne, you weren't raped?

                    JAZMYNE
(Looking ashamed) No. For so
many years, I just wanted to
be liked, accepted. I never
knew my father. My mother left
me when I was five. What kind
of mother leaves her child?
When I met Yadeh, he treated
me like I was special. He
erased all of my problems away.

                    JAZMYNE (Cont'd)
          He has this way of touching
          you. And when I was with him,
          I felt important. And I
          thought by doing that, he
          would continue to love me.

Katie is sitting in disbelief.

                    KATIE
          That wasn't love that Yadeh
          had. You need to tell Josh.

CG: Two weeks later.

INT. PHYSICAL REHAB CENTER - DAY

Josh is walking down the hall on crutches with his
mother. Jazmyne has a bouquet of flowers that she
bought for him. She walks up smiling. Josh's mother
has an indifferent look, but eventually smiles.

                    MRS. SHEPHERD
          We've been truly blessed this
          afternoon. Hey, baby. (looking
          at Jazmyne)

                    JAZMYNE
          Hey, Mama Shep.

                    MRS. SHEPHERD
          How you doin'?

                    JAZMYNE
          Pretty good. Hey, Josh!

Josh and Jazmyne hug.

                    JOSH
          Hey, Jazz. I started to wonder
          about you. I left you a
          million messages.

                    JAZMYNE
          I know. I know. I had to take
          time out to get things in
          order with me, life and all.

                    JOSH
          I understand. (pushes her)
          It's good to see you.

Josh looks at his mother.

                    MRS. SHEPHERD
          Jazmyne, I'm glad you're here.
          I gotta run to the church for
          a couple of hours. Can you
          finish his rehab training up?

                    JAZMYNE
          I don't…

                    MRS. SHEPHERD
          Child, all you have to do is
          walk with him. Just walk
          with him.

                    JAZMYNE
          Yes, ma'am.

                MRS. SHEPHERD
        I'll be back later to check
        on you. (talking to Josh)Bye,
        babies.

Kisses Josh and Jazmyne.

They begin walking and nothing is said.

                JAZMYNE
        They treatin' you aight up
        in here?

                JOSH
        It's OK. Food is nasty.

                JAZMYNE
        How you coming?

                JOSH
        OK, but I am really worried
        about you.

                JAZMYNE
        I've been going through my
        own troubles the last couple
        of weeks.

                JOSH
        I figured…. Like to share?

                JAZMYNE
        Not ready yet, but…

                JOSH
        Yeah? (They stop walking.)

>   JAZMYNE
>   Something that has been eating
>   at me for many years, but now…
>   I have peace. I've accepted
>   Christ into my life.

>   JOSH
>   Serious?

>   JAZMYNE
>   Yep!

>   JOSH
>   Get outta here!

>   JAZMYNE
>   No kiddin'.

>   JOSH
>   Jazmyne Greer, that's… that's
>   wonderful. I'm so happy! I
>   don't need these crutches
>   anymore. I can….

Josh walks a couple of steps and falls.

INT. DANCE ROOM STUDIO - DAY - FOX THEATRE

Jazmyne walks into the dance studio. She walks past
a lot of dancers that she has danced with years
back. She still has her street clothes on and meets
up with Katie.

>   JAZMYNE
>   Hey, Katie.

                    KATIE
          Glad you could make it.
          Remember these days?
          The people?

                   JAZMYNE
          All good memories.

                    KATIE
          I got some warm ups in
          my locker.

                   JAZMYNE
          For what? Why are we here
          anyway?

                    KATIE
          To go back to your first love.
          Hey, Curtis! (Man walks by.)
          Remember when we had our convo
          about ministry?

Two little girls walk in the room playing together.

                    GIRLS
          Hey, Ms. Katie.

They walk and snuggle under Katie's arms.

                    KATIE
          This is my ministry.

Ten more girls come in running.

                    KATIE
          Stop running. Slow down!

                    GIRLS
        Hi, Mrs. Katie!

                    KATIE
        Everyone circle up around me,
        quickly, quickly, quickly.
        That is not a circle—give me
        a circle. That's better.
        Good afternoon!

                    GIRLS
        Hi, Mrs. Katie.

                    KATIE
        Everybody, we have a special
        visitor with us today. This is
        Ms. Jazmyne. Everybody say hi
        to Ms. Jazmyne.

                    GIRLS
        Hi, Ms. Jazmyne!

Two girls in the back of the group begin whispering
to one another.

                    KATIE
        Today we are going to learn to
        do some difficult ballet moves.
        Everybody familiar with ballet,
        right? Uh, ladies in the back,
        no talking when I'm talking.
        You care to share what you're
        whispering in the back?

                    TWO GIRLS
        No.

                    KATIE
          Please share. You felt it was
          important enough to talk when
          I'm talking.

                    SHULA
          We know her, we've seen her
          before. She's a video dancer
          for Yadeh Ya.

Everyone, including parents, looks around at each
other. Jazmyne looks around and is embarrassed. She
proceeds to walk out.

                    KATIE
          Ladies, please begin stretching.
          We'll be right back.

Katie immediately follows after her.

                    KATIE
          Look, making this life
          transition is not going to be
          easy. One of the first things
          that you're gonna have to
          do is…

                    JAZMYNE
          I know… convince them that I
          am a different person.

                    KATIE
          Convincing means you're still
          living the life of your past.
          Show them by how you live your
          life now. Not with words, but

                    KATIE (Cont'd)
by living. It's a hard and
long road, but I know you
can do it.

                    JAZMYNE
What do you want me to do?

                    KATIE
Teach them dancing and
about God.

                    JAZMYNE
I don't know enough to teach
them about God.

                    KATIE
You teach them as you learn.
Don't you want to help with
the girls?

                    JAZMYNE
Sure. What I gotta do?

                    KATIE
Learn as you go.

                    JAZMYNE
It seems like you have all the
answers. Have you ever done
anything wrong?

Katie puts her hand on Jazmyne's shoulder.

                    KATIE
     We don't have enough hours in
     the day for me to begin telling
     you what God delivered me from.

They both laugh and begin walking back inside
of the dance studio. The parents are looking
concerned.

                    KATIE
     Ms. Jazz has agreed to join
     our group. And yes, Shula, she
     was a dancer for a big time
     rapper and has done some other
     things she isn't the most
     proud of. Raise your hand if
     you've done something that
     you're not proud of, something
     wrong?

Katie points to young girl.

                    KATIE
     Do you care to share what
     you did?

                    GIRL ONE
     Uhh… no.

                    KATIE
     OK, that's fair. Does anybody
     care to share? OK, Morgan.

                    MORGAN
          I ate my mommy's cookies when
          she said I couldn't have
          anymore.

                    KATIE
          And you, Stephanie?

Pastor Sparks walks in.

                    STEPHANIE
          When we were at the mall, I
          went to the toy store.

                    KATIE
          What's so bad about that? Did
          your mommy or daddy know where
          you were?

                    STEPHANIE
          No.

                    KATIE
          OK, so we all did something
          that we shouldn't have done.
          But guess what? Guess what?

                    ALL GIRLS
          What?

                    KATIE
          That's why Jesus died for us,
          to pay for all of our sins
          and for the things that we
          shouldn't do. Nobody's perfect
          but Him. So when you do

                    KATIE (Cont'd)
something you're not supposed
to, or you're not proud of
later, you need to pray for
forgiveness. And don't do it
again. (looking at Jazmyne)

                ALL GIRLS
OK.

                    KATIE
Let me tell you some other
things that Ms. Jazmyne has
done. Do you know she was the
lead dancer at the Atlanta
Ballet Company for years?
Did you know she has danced
all over the world, in front
of thousands of people? For
Kings, presidents, little
princesses. And now, she's
on fire for God.

Girls get excited.

                    KATIE
So, ladies, let's welcome Ms.
Jazmyne into the Angels praise
troupe!

All of the girls run up to Jazmyne and hug her.
Pastor smiles and walks out. Jazmyne looks down at
the two girls that recognized her earlier.

                    JAZMYNE
        I see I'm a have to keep tabs
        on ya'll two! If you knew who
        I was that means you was
        watching something you
        shouldn't have.

                    NATALIE
        Busted! (pointing to Shula)I
        told you!

                    JAZMYNE
        What's your name?

                    NATALIE
        I'm Natalie and this is Shula.

                    JAZMYNE
        Alright, Natalie and Shula,
        I want you two to be my
        right hand!

Girls look at one another and give each other a
high five.

INT. JOSH'S APARTMENT - AFTERNOON

Jazmyne is coming for a surprise visit to Josh's
apartment. Mrs. Shepherd answers the door.

                MRS. SHEPHERD
        Hey, Jazz! How you doin'?

                    JAZMYNE
        I'm good, Mama Shep. You?

                    MRS. SHEPHERD
I'm alive. I'm doing real good.
Josh's in the back. Come on in.

                    JAZMYNE
How you enjoying Atlanta?

                    MRS. SHEPHERD
I don't like the malls. It's
too many people for me.
And the traffic…. What you do
when you gotta pee? I need to
put me a cup in the car, just
in case.

                    JAZMYNE
You a mess. (both laugh)

                    MRS. SHEPHERD
You look different. I like it.

                    JAZMYNE
I am different.

                    MRS. SHEPHERD
Whatever it is, keep it up.
You have a certain glow about
yourself. You and Josh have
been spending a lot of time
together.

                    JAZMYNE
Yeah.

                    MRS. SHEPHERD
Ya'll courtin'?

                        JAZMYNE
Mama Shep, I'm falling for him.
He's been the only one in my
life that I can truly say will
care and love me with a sincere
heart. We haven't really talked
about our feelings, but he's
gotta know. And I know he's
liked me since grade school.
I just had to do a lot of
growing up to appreciate him.
Mama… I think I love him.

                    MRS. SHEPHERD
Don't hurt my boy.

                        JAZMYNE
I'm not.

                    MRS. SHEPHERD
Well, don't. All I've got to
say is, I've seen first hand how
you've treated him over the
years, how many times you've
broken his heart. Don't hurt
my baby.

                        JAZMYNE
Mrs. Shepherd.

                    MRS. SHEPHERD
I've loved you unconditionally
and have accepted you as my own.
Just don't play with him if
you're not serious.

                    JAZMYNE
          I won't. Really.

Josh walks in.

                    JOSH
          What's my two favorite ladies
          talking about?

They look at one another.

                    JOSH
          Hey, Jazz! This is a nice
          surprise. Hey, come back in
          the back. I want to show you
          something.

He grabs her hand and both walk in the back room.

INT. JOSH'S PHOTO REC ROOM - DAY

Walls are decorated with all types of photos that
Josh has taken throughout the years.

                    JAZMYNE
          I feel honored. I've never
          been back here before.

                    JOSH
          Well, things are a little
          different now.

They look at each other. Jazmyne looks around the
room at the different pictures. Every photo seems
symbolic, having an underlying tone or meaning.
She is truly in awe of his talent in photography.

                          JAZMYNE
            You truly have an eye.

Jazmyne looks at a certain picture.

                          JAZMYNE
            You took this at the hospital.
            It's the hallway where Papa was.

                          JOSH
            That's my best photo yet!

                          JAZMYNE
            It's a hallway.

                          JOSH
            Closer. Look closer.

                          JAZMYNE
            It's just a photo of patients
            and doctors working.

                          JOSH
            OK.

Jazmyne keeps looking but doesn't see anything that
captures her attention.

                          JAZMYNE
            It's a lady crying.

                          JOSH
            Yes. Still don't get it?

                          JAZMYNE
            Sorry.

                    JOSH
Look closer. It's a hallway,
but you see the lady crying?
(pauses) She was crying, while
the doctors where wheeling out
her husband, who I later found
out died in the ER.

                  JAZMYNE
Sad.

                    JOSH
But wait, look closer. In the
window.

                  JAZMYNE
I don't see it, just tell me.

                    JOSH
A woman just delivered a baby.
The beginning of one life and
the end of another. All on the
same hallway. That's symbolism.
I don't just take pictures,
I look for the beauty in each
shot. Enough with symbolism—I
was digging through some old
photos and I ran across this.

It is a photo of them as kids singing and dancing
together at an elementary talent show.

                    JOSH
Remember that?

                    JAZMYNE
          Do I remember? We was the bomb!

                     JOSH
          I remember that song too! Come
          on, get in position.

Josh continues to sing while Jazmyne dances around
the room and laughing. Jazmyne stops and listens
while Josh continues to sing.

Mrs. Shepherd tiptoes back and peeks in the door.

                     JOSH
          (sings) I see us in the park
          strolling the summer days of
          imaginings in my head. And
          words from our hearts, told
          only to the wind felt even
          without being said. I don't
          want to bore you with my
          trouble. But there's something
          'bout your love that makes me
          weak and knocks me off my feet.
          There's something 'bout your
          love that makes me weak and
          knocks me off my feet.

                  MRS. SHEPHERD
          (whispers) Get it, boy.

Josh starts moving his hand over her body.

                  MRS. SHEPHERD
          Whoa, whoa, don't get it, boy.

She begins making noises in the hallway.

                    JOSH
          I've been waiting for this
          moment since I first met you.
          I've always thought that you
          were the most beautiful woman
          I've ever seen.

Jazmyne blushes.

                    JAZMYNE
          I don't know what to say.

                    JOSH
          I've really enjoyed our time
          lately.

                    JAZMYNE
          Me too! But hey, Josh, I gotta
          tell you something.

                    JOSH
          You don't feel the same? I know.

                    JAZMYNE
          (holding Josh's face) Josh,
          you have no idea how much I am
          enjoying this. You are truly
          an angel. You are the only man
          that I know that accepts me
          for me.

                    JOSH
          What is it?

                    JAZMYNE
I...

                    JOSH
I'll lose weight.

                    JAZMYNE
It has nothing to do with you.
It's me.

                    JOSH
Oh, I've heard that before.
You're too nice, Josh. I think
of you more as a brother than
a boyfriend.

                    JAZMYNE
Hear me out. I...

                  MRS. SHEPHERD
I gotta come check up on you
two. First I heard talking,
then I heard some singing and
bumping 'round, then it got
quiet. When Josh was little,
I always knew he was up to
something when he got quiet.
I knew he was probably looking
at some dirty magazines from
the neighborhood kids, from
Norman.

Everybody laughs.

                    EVERYONE
Norman!

                    JOSH
Must you tell everything?

                 MRS. SHEPHERD
I mean.

                    JOSH
I mean, really, something has
to be sacred.

                 MRS. SHEPHERD
Dirty magazines? Sacred?
(laughs)

                    JOSH
OK, bad choice of words.

                  JAZMYNE
Well, actually, I already knew
about the dirty magazines.

                    JOSH
You knew too?

                  JAZMYNE
Well, yeah. Everybody knew.
It wasn't a secret. I heard
you tell Carl Twyman.

                    JOSH
He told you?

                  JAZMYNE
Well, no. Maggie Johnson.

                         JOSH
            Maggie Johnson? Who told her?

                        JAZMYNE
            Carl told Benji, and Benji…

                         JOSH
            Benji? Benji Hooks?

                        JAZMYNE
            Just know that your secret
            wasn't really a secret. It was
            out there. We just acted like
            we didn't know.

                         JOSH
            Well, let me put this out
            there, Mama. Me and Jazz are
            an item. (looking at Jazmyne)
            Can I say that?

Jazmyne nods her head "yes" and smiles.

                      MRS. SHEPHERD
            An item? Did you ask her? Do
            grown folks ask each other
            nowadays or do they just
            assume? Did he ask you, girl?

                        JAZMYNE
            Well, not exactly. But it's
            cool.

Mrs. Shepherd looks at Josh.

                    JOSH
        Jazmyne, will you…. Hold on.

Josh grabs a pen and paper, scribbles on it, and
holds it up. It says, "Will you be my Valentimes?"

                  JAZMYNE
        You so silly. Yes!

They hug.

                  JAZMYNE
        This is my new beau!

Mrs. Shepherd smiles.

INT. DANCE STUDIO - DAY

Girls are practicing various moves in unison to
beautiful symphonic music, which is a beautiful
sight to witness.

<music slowly fades out>

                     KATIE
              That was so beautiful. Lasha,
              make sure that you lift your
              right leg as high as you can
              at the very end.(pauses)OK, I
              have wonderful news, and I
              have more wonderful news. The
              wonderful news: I have just
              accepted a position into the
              Illustrious Broadway Dance
              Company. I will finally dance
              on Broadway, as well as other

                    KATIE (Cont'd)
cities throughout the country!
Now the more wonderful news:
Since I have to move to New
York, Ms. Jazmyne will take
over as your lead instructor,
starting the next rehearsal.

                    GIRLS
That's not wonderful—we want
you. Stay here.

                 MORE GIRLS
Yeah, don't go.

                    KATIE
I know, babies, but this is
something I've been praying
about for some time now. And
when God moves, you gotta go
or you'll miss that blessing
out of fear.

Jazmyne is speechless.

                  JAZMYNE
Uh, I can't do this.
They're right.

                    KATIE
Nonsense. You're already
doing it.

                  JAZMYNE
When you leaving?

                    KATIE
Friday.

                    JAZMYNE
Friday? Thanks for the advance
notice.

                    KATIE
No worries. You'll be fine.
You can stay at the apartment.
I have it paid up for three
months.

                    JAZMYNE
I need you.

                    KATIE
You don't. You're ready. Plus,
there's always a phone. Don't
hesitate to call me for
anything.

They look at each other and hug.

INT. JOSH'S APARTMENT - NIGHT

Josh and Jazmyne are watching the History Channel
about the Holocaust.

                    JOSH
Now see, if I woulda been
there, a whole lot of things
would be different. Hitler
ain't nothin'. I'd handled him,
trust me.

                    JAZMYNE
        Sure you would've. I'm sure we
        can say the same thing about
        slavery until you got hit with
        a whip!

                    JOSH
        I know, it's so easy to say
        what you would've done after
        things have past.

                    JAZMYNE
        See what else is on.

Josh flips through the stations.

                    JAZMYNE
        Wait a minute. Go back.

The station is showing a video of Yadeh and Misha.
Both Josh and Jazmyne continue to watch and are
engrossed by it. The video ends and a commercial
comes on.

                    JOSH
        You miss him? It? The life?

                    JAZMYNE
        This life is so much sweeter
        than I could've ever imagined.

                    JOSH
        Good answer.

                    JAZMYNE
    I love being with you. That's
    for real. (pauses) You remember
    a couple of weeks ago I said I
    had to tell you something and
    never got around to it?

Josh perks up.

                    JOSH
    Yeah… What is it?

                    JAZMYNE
    Do you remember on that day of
    the video shoot?

Josh just looks at her.

                    JAZMYNE
    I… I wasn't… raped.

                    JOSH
    What do you mean? Of course
    you were. You filed a police
    report and everything. You
    told me you did.

                    JAZMYNE
    No, I didn't. You did, and I
    never corrected you. I'm sorry
    for not telling you.

                    JOSH
    Wait a minute… Are you telling
    me you wanted what happened
    to you?

                    JAZMYNE
          No, but…

                    JOSH
          But what? Either you did or
          you didn't.

                    JAZMYNE
          Yeah, no. I didn't but…

                    JOSH
          I almost got my head knocked
          off because of it.

                    JAZMYNE
          Wait a second. Let me explain.

                    JOSH
          I don't…. Shut up…. I don't…

                    JAZMYNE
          I have an…

                    JOSH
          I know what you have. What you
          have is a problem.

Silence enters the room.

                    JOSH
          Look, it's getting late. I
          think you need to go.

                    JAZMYNE
          So that's that, huh? You won't
          hear me out?

Josh walks her to the door.

                    JOSH
          31.

                    JAZMYNE
          (sighs) 31, what's 31?

                    JOSH
          This makes the 31st time where
          you've broken my heart and,
          you know, I'm tired of being
          a fool.

                    JAZMYNE
          You're not a fool. (walks out)

INT. YADEH'S BEDROOM - NIGHT

Yadeh is having another terrible nightmare. It
is a montage of Jazmyne being baptized, Yadeh
being molested, and rattling of key chains. Misha
is right beside him when he wakes up abruptly. She
tries to console him, but he pushes her off of him.

                    YADEH
          I'm aight! Stop!

INT. DANCE STUDIO - AFTERNOON

Jazmyne is walking through the rows of dancers and
correcting postures and various moves.

                    JAZMYNE
          Where are your hearts? You're
          praising. But ya'll are just
          going through the motions.
          Raise your hands higher!
          Yes, yes!

<Music ends>

                    JAZMYNE
          Very good ladies, very good.
          We are off to a very good start.
          But remember at the end of the
          year is our big event. You
          should think about it every
          day and how to get better every
          day. Who wants to close us out?

Most of the girls raise their hands. Jazmyne points
to Shula.

                    JAZMYNE
          Go for it.

                     SHULA
          Lord, thank you for another
          day we have together. Bless
          everybody and their families
          and a safe trip home. Amen.

                   ALL GIRLS
          Amen.

All girls start running to the dressing room.

                    JAZMYNE
          Slow down.

Shula and Natalie stagger behind. Jazmyne walks up
behind them and puts her arms around them both.

                    JAZMYNE
          Why ya'll moving slow? You've
          been moving like this all
          practice.

                    NATALIE
          Our 8th grade dance is next
          week.

                    JAZMYNE
          What's so bad about that?

                    SHULA
          She's sad because...

They stop walking.

                    NATALIE
          Shula...

                    SHULA
          Natalie.

                    NATALIE
          What? Somebody needs to know.
          She doesn't have anything to
          wear.

Jazmyne looks at them both.

                    JAZMYNE
          Is that it?

                    NATALIE
          This is major. Andre is going
          to be there.

                    JAZMYNE
          Andre? This is a about some
          little knuckle-head boy.

                    NATALIE
          Well, no, sorta.

                    SHULA
          He's goofy lookin'. Ms.
          Jazmyne, he got a big head.

                    NATALIE
          No, he doesn't. He is so cute.

                    JAZMYNE
          Look, you are too young to be
          thinking about boys. Just
          focus on God and your books.
          Please trust me. I know.

                    NATALIE
          Please, how old are you?
          Like 50?

                    JAZMYNE
          50?

Jazmyne chases Natalie around the studio and
catches her.

                    JAZMYNE
But for real, I'm sure Andre is cute and all, but
the Andres of the world will always be there. My
grandfather told me if you really like him and
he likes you, he'll be around. Listen to me now;
believe me later on, in the future. Now does that
change how you feel about going to this dance?

                    NATALIE
          Uhh, no.

                    JAZMYNE
          Let's go shopping.

                    NATALIE
          For real?

                    JAZMYNE
          (looking at Shula) You too!

                    SHULA
          Get out!

                    JAZMYNE
          Ask your parents first, but
          yeah.

INT. DEPARTMENT STORE - DAY

Natalie, Shula, and Jazmyne walk through a
cluttered department store browsing through
the racks.

                    NATALIE
          How much can I spend?

                         JAZMYNE
              Don't go crazy!

                   NATALIE AND SHULA
              For real Ms. Jazz?

Jazmyne looks at the two girls. The girls get
excited and start jumping up and down. They
immediately take off.

                         JAZMYNE
              Don't go too far. I'll be by
              the dressing room.

Jazmyne walks to the dressing room to find a seat.
She runs into Misha. Misha is leaving with an arm
full of clothes. They share an awkward moment.

                         JAZMYNE
              Misha?

                          MISHA
              Jazmyne.

                       BOTH WOMEN
              Hey.

They exchange and awkward hug.

                         JAZMYNE
              What you up to?

                          MISHA
              Just doing a little shopping.

                    JAZMYNE
          A little?

Both laugh.

                    MISHA
          How you been?

                    JAZMYNE
          I've been doin' good. A lot
          has changed since we last spoke.

                    MISHA
          You look different.

                    JAZMYNE
          I've been seeing you on TV.

                    MISHA
          Yeah, life has been pretty good.

                    JAZMYNE
          I'm glad I ran into you.

                    MISHA
          Yeah?

                    JAZMYNE
          Yeah.

The two girls walk up with an armful of clothes.

                    JAZMYNE
          Ladies, this is…

                    GIRLS
          Misha.

                    JAZMYNE
          I shoulda figured.

Everyone laughs.

                    JAZMYNE
          I see somebody still has been
          watchin' MTV.

Everyone laughs.

                    GIRLS
          Hi, Misha.

                    MISHA
          Hey, I like those outfits.
          They're cute.

She grabs an outfit and holds it up.

                    JAZMYNE
          We gotta see them on first.

The girls run back in the dressing room.

                    JAZMYNE
          They are a part of a ministry
          that I run.

                    MISHA
          Ministry? Yeah, I heard you
          got real religious.

                    JAZMYNE
No, I didn't get religious, I
found Christ. I know that this
may sound crazy, but when I
was with Yadeh, I thought that
I had everything. I did. I did
have THINGS. But something
still wasn't right. I didn't
have peace. And on that day
when everything went down, I
surrendered my life to Christ.
At the hospital parking lot.

                    MISHA
Hmm.

                    JAZMYNE
Misha, I've been where you are.
I've done what you're doing
and more. Yadeh's probably
paying for all those clothes.
Girl, he's gonna take your
soul. He's not at peace. The
constant nightmares he has.
Times where he just seems
where he's carrying the world
on his shoulders. And he'll
step on you in the process.

                    MISHA
Girl, please. This sounds all
good and all. You just mad
because you's a hoe and Yadeh
didn't want you anymore.

                    JAZMYNE
        Is that what you think? I was
        on a path of destruction. But
        there's a better way.

                    MISHA
        That's what most used up hoes
        like you say.

Both girls come out of the dressing room and join
the conversation.

                    JAZMYNE
        Hey, that's pretty.

                    NATALIE
        Did I just hear you call Ms.
        Jazz a hoe? First of all, with
        your tired weave, nobody calls
        Ms. Jazz names and think they
        can just walk away. Hold on,
        let me change. I don't care if
        you on TV, you 'bout to get it!

                    JAZMYNE
        Natalie, Natalie, please calm
        down.

                    MISHA
        Oh, so this is the ministry
        you have? Your little church
        girl got more fire than you.

Misha proceeds to walk away.

                    JAZMYNE
          (looking at Natalie) OK, that
          was real ghetto. Natalie, you
          are representing Christ. I
          know it's hard at times but
          you always stay calm and
          collected.

                    NATALIE
          But Ms. Jazz, she called
          you a….

                    JAZMYNE
          Trust me, I heard it the first
          five times. So what? I gotta
          fight her? I've been called
          much worse. Enough with that—
          let's see what you have on.

Jazmyne holds the girls' shoulders.

                    JAZMYNE
          This is you. (Jazmyne looks at
          Shula.) What else you got?

EXT. OLD COUNTRY ROAD - MIDDAY

Jazmyne and Pastor Sparks share a moment while
walking down an old country Georgia road.

                    JAZMYNE
          So that's what happened.

                    PASTOR SPARKS
          I'm glad that you had time to
          meet with me.

                    JAZMYNE
          Sure thing, but uh, couldn't
          we have met at the church. You
          trying to get romantic on me?

                  PASTOR SPARKS
          Don't flatter yourself.

                    JAZMYNE
          Sorry, I'm just used to men
          always wanting something.

                  PASTOR SPARKS
          I understand. But that's the
          past.

Silence comes. They keep walking.

                  PASTOR SPARKS
          I wanted to take time out to
          say how grateful I am that you
          joined the ministry. God is
          doing some awesome things.
          How's everything going?

                    JAZMYNE
          Good, but tough. Those girls
          are stubborn, I mean.

Both laugh.

                  PASTOR SPARKS
          My sentiments exactly. Just
          stay encouraged and let me know
          if there's anything you need.

                    JAZMYNE
OK.

                 PASTOR SPARKS
Jazmyne, I haven't been
completely open with you,
and I need your help with
something.

                    JAZMYNE
Sure, what is it?

                 PASTOR SPARKS
I have a pretty good knowledge
of your past. You started at
the Atlanta Ballet for many
years, then danced in a number
of rap videos, calendars and
dated Yadeh Ya.

                    JAZMYNE
Yes.

                 PASTOR SPARKS
Did Yadeh ever speak of his
father?

                    JAZMYNE
He would always change the
subject and get very angry
whenever I asked. I remember
him saying that he got kicked
out while he was in high
school. I do remember when we
were at the radio station,
this was some time ago, his

                    JAZMYNE (Cont'd)
father called up to the
station to talk with him and
he started yelling. I don't
know what was said, but I know
he was furious.

                    PASTOR SPARKS
He told me if he ever saw me
again, he'd kill me.

Jazmyne stops and is astonished.

                    PASTOR SPARKS
Yes, before then, it had been
many years.

                    JAZMYNE
Hold on… You? So what
happened? Why does he hate you?

                    PASTOR SPARKS
Long time ago, I didn't know
the Lord. I just acted like it
in public. I remember Katie
telling the girls that
everyone has done something
that they aren't proud of. I
had a sickness no prescription
could ever cure. And only by
allowing Christ in and a lot of
counseling, I've changed. I
had to break that generational
curse passed down from my
father. I'm still ashamed.
This is my testimony that I

PASTER SPARKS (Cont'd)
share often with offenders.
But thank you, Lord. The church
is full of former killers,
rapists, prostitutes, thieves,
and the biggest hypocrites you
will ever see. But the beauty
in it is they acknowledge that
they can't make it on their
own. They look to Christ.

JAZMYNE
I wasn't ready for that,
Pastor. What did the church
say about this?

PASTOR SPARKS
Well, I've only been pastor
for one year officially. The
deacon board is reviewing me.
There are several members that
never wanted me here because
of that, and are still being
persistent at letting me go.

JAZMYNE
How do you feel about that?

PASTOR SPARKS
Whatever God's will is, I'm
comfortable with that. How do
you feel about it?

JAZMYNE
I don't know. I guess it's
alright. Let me think about it.

Al Smith

They continue walking.

                    JAZMYNE
          You said that you needed
          something from me? See, you
          did want something! (laughs)

                    PASTOR SPARKS
          I need to get in contact with
          him. Yadeh.

                    JAZMYNE
          Sure thing. I'll give you his
          cell when we get back to the
          church. It's been a little
          while now. He might have
          changed his number. You know
          celebrities change their
          numbers all the time. Are
          you scared to speak to him,
          knowing he threatened you?

                    PASTOR SPARKS
          Jazmyne, I am covered by the
          blood. I'm not worried. No
          weapons formed against me
          shall prosper. Have you heard
          that before?

                    JAZMYNE
          All the time.

                    PASTOR SPARKS
          It was good talking with you.
          I'll see you back at the church.

                    JAZMYNE
What's going on? Where you
going? You gonna just leave me
here? I don't get it.

                 PASTOR SPARKS
You aren't alone.

Pastor Sparks points behind her, and Jazmyne turns
around. She sees a blanket with a note on top of
it. She walks up and sits down on the blanket. She
holds the letter up and looks at Pastor Sparks. He
smiles and begins walking back toward the church.
She opens the letter.

                   JOSH'S V.O.
My beautiful Jazzy, it's funny
how a story can change by one
incident, one word, or one
wrong conversation. I never
heard you out that day. In
many ways I kinda knew what
you were going to tell me. I
swore to myself that I would
never talk to you again. But
as each day went by, my heart
has longed just to hear you,
to see your beautiful smile,
just to share time and space
with you. I've been doing a
lot of thinking, and I've come
to a conclusion: I can't live
without you. I can't breathe
without you. Love is forgiving
when you don't want to forgive.
Love is kind when you want to

Al Smith

                    JOSH'S V.O. (Cont'd)
          be mean and spiteful. And
          spite is not how I chose to
          fill my heart. I love you, more
          than I could ever express.
          Jazmyne Greer, we've been
          performing together since the
          second grade, and I can't see
          sharing my life's stage with
          anyone else but you. Will you
          marry me?

Josh steps from behind a tree and begins singing.

                    JOSH
          You are so beautiful to me.
          You are so beautiful to me.
          You are so beautiful to me,
          can't you see. You're
          everything that I'd hope for.
          You're everything I need.
          You are so beautiful to me.

<Soft music plays in the background>

                    JOSH
          Right before your Papa died,
          he made me promise that I'd
          take care of you.

INT. HOSPITAL ROOM - FLASHBACK

Papa lays weak in his hospital bed with Josh at
his side.

                        JOSH'S V.O.
"Son," he said, "when my days
on this earth have come to an
end, I want you to look after
her. Be that light in the
midst of the dark hallway she
has chosen. Please. Let me
rest in peace, so that I know
someone will guide her way
back home. Will you do that,
son?"

Josh nods his head "yes."

                        JOSH'S V.O.
"Bless you."

EXT. OLD COUNTRY ROAD - MIDDAY

                        JOSH
And after that night at the
video shoot, I felt like I let
him and you down.

                        JAZMYNE
I wasn't…

                        JOSH
You aren't hearing what I'm
saying. I want to take care of
you. Let me do that. Marry me.

Jazmyne nods her head "yes."

Al Smith

EXT. WEDDING SCENE - DAY

<"You Are So Beautiful" music continues softly in
the background>

Josh and Jazmyne are standing in front of the same
creek with only a handful of people. Natalie,
Shula, and Katie are in their wedding party. They
exchange vows. Butterflies are released. Katie hands
Jazmyne her jar. Jazmyne seems perplexed because
she didn't think that Katie knew about her
butterfly.

Jazmyne opens the jar and the butterfly slowly moves
and flies out of the jar.

                    PAPA'S V.O.
              You never want to keep your
              own soul. It's God's.

MONTAGE

- Jazmyne dancing with girls.

- Josh and Jazmyne walking through the grocery
  store.

- Misha dancing in another video.

- Misha becoming neglected by Yadeh.

- Pastor Sparks sitting amongst the deacons at a
  table and there is a serious argument.

- Josh and Jazmyne in bed and the clock reads 4:30
  AM. Jazz gets up and runs to the bathroom to

throw up. Josh doesn't budge. He's still sleep.

- Jazmyne teaching girls in front of a crowd.

- Jazmyne walking out of the bathroom with a
  pregnancy test. She looks up at Josh and starts
  smiling. They hug.

INT. JOSH AND JAZMYNE'S BACKYARD - EARLY MORNING

- MONTHS LATER

<Music "Grateful">

Jazmyne is stretching early in the morning. Josh
is walking around the house quietly and discovers
Jazmyne stretching. He is in awe of Jazmyne's
beauty. He quickly grabs his camera and begins
snapping shots. Jazmyne is in her own world with
her eyes closed and does not know that he's taking
pictures.

INT. RADIO STATION RECEPTIONIST AREA - DAY

Jazmyne walks into the lobby with Natalie and Shula
and approach the front desk.

                    RECEPTIONIST
          Jazmyne Greer.

                      JAZMYNE
          Shepherd… Jazmyne Shepherd.
          (holds up wedding ring finger)

The telephones are ringing constantly.

                    RECEPTIONIST
I see somebody has been busy.
Congrats!

                    JAZMYNE
(rubbing her stomach)
Thank you!

                    RECEPTIONIST
And who do we have with you?

                    JAZMYNE
This is Shula and Natalie.

            SHULA AND NATALIE
Hi.

                    RECEPTIONIST
(holds up her hand) WTTX.
How may I direct your call?

                    RECEPTIONIST
I'm sorry, things are getting
a little hectic. Who you here
to see?

                    JAZMYNE
Flex One.

                    RECEPTIONIST
You have an appointment?

                    JAZMYNE
No.

> RECEPTIONIST
> No problem. Hold on. Let me
> see if he's in the studio.
> (dials)Hey, babe, I got Jazmyne
> here to see you. OK. (looking
> at Jazmyne) He'll be out in a
> minute, if you want to have
> a seat.

The girls walk around the room and look at the
photos on the wall. Flex One walks out moments
later.

> FLEX ONE
> What's the deal, peoples? Look
> at you! How are you?

They hug.

> JAZMYNE
> I'm good. Good to see you. Oh,
> and this is Shula and Natalie.

> FLEX ONE
> Hey, babies, come on back.

INT. STUDIO - DAY

All four walk into a studio.

> FLEX ONE
> So I heard about the nasty
> break up with you and Yadeh.
> You aight?

                    JAZMYNE
        I am so good right now.

                    FLEX ONE
        Yeah?

                    JAZMYNE
        I'm taking time out to get my
        life in order. I've found
        Christ now: I've dedicated my
        life to Him, which brings me
        to why I'm here.

                    FLEX ONE
        That is? I thought you came
        to holler at me since you and
        Yadeh are done, but I see
        somebody else has beat me to
        the punch! (laughs)

                    JAZMYNE
        You so silly. I'm running a
        ministry for little girls,
        young ladies and praise dancing.

                    FLEX ONE
        OK?

                    JAZMYNE
        I'm so excited about this
        ministry and the girls that I
        wanted to get on-air with you
        to talk about our upcoming
        performance we are having.

                    FLEX ONE
        (shifts body uncomfortably)
        I see.

                    JAZMYNE
        And you said, when I was here
        last time, that I can come
        back and get on the air
        whenever I wanted.

                    FLEX ONE
        (looks at girls and pauses)
        Ya'll like candy?

                SHULA AND NATALIE
        Yeah.

                    FLEX ONE
        Go back to the receptionist
        desk and ask Lydia to get you
        some M&Ms. Jazz will be out
        in a minute. Wait there.

                    NATALIE
        Nah, I'm OK. Candy is bad for
        your teeth.

Jazmyne gives Natalie a stern look.

                    NATALIE
        OK. Come on girl.

They get up and leave the room.

                    FLEX ONE
        You can't be serious?

                         JAZMYNE
          What do you mean?

                        FLEX ONE
          You are serious. Do you know
          how the radio station stays
          alive?

                         JAZMYNE
          I'm sure you're about to
          tell me.

                        FLEX ONE
          Advertisers.

                         JAZMYNE
          What does that have to do with
          what I'm asking you to do?

                        FLEX ONE
          Advertisers won't pay if
          we have no audience. Our
          listeners will tune us out
          if we have you and the little
          girls on air talking about
          God and Jesus.

                         JAZMYNE
          Somebody will listen.

                        FLEX ONE
          But our advertisers don't want
          to pay for it. It's cute and
          all, but I can't do it.

                    JAZMYNE
Yes, you can. You are the man.
The city loves you. If you say
something, people will listen.
Let them know God is about to
do something big in this city.

                    FLEX ONE
That's flattering. You have
such a way with men. But I'm
not buying it. I'm the man in
this city because I spent
years building my name and
paying dues. I did. God did
nothing. Sorry, I can't help
you on this one. My shift is
about to start. Please see
yourself out. (begins pushing
buttons)

INT. RECEPTIONIST AREA

Jazmyne walks into the lobby and whisks past the
receptionist.

                    JAZMYNE
OK, ladies, ready?

                    NATALIE AND SHULA
Where we going? I thought we
were gonna be on the radio?

                    JAZMYNE
Not today. We gotta keep
moving.

Al Smith

CU of receptionist's face.

                    RECEPTIONIST
          Bye.

Montage of Jazmyne going to different radio and
television stations asking to help promote the
event and being denied.

EXT. CREEK SCENE - DAY - FLASHBACK

Jazmyne is walking into a country creek where
she is met with a pastor in an all white robe.
She proceeds to get baptized in the water. When
she is lifted from the water by the pastor, she
wipes her eyes. The clouds separate and formulate
the word "forgiven." She smiles. All at once a
butterfly swoops down and lands on the tips of her
fingers. She looks at Pastor Sparks. Pastor's face
is finally revealed, it's Yadeh's father.

INT. YADEH'S BEDROOM

Yadeh is awakened by the flashback/dream. Misha is
in bed with him and tries to console him.

                    MISHA
          You alright?

                    YADEH
          Get off me. I'm fine.

CU of Misha's face. Misha looks troubled.

CG: One Week Later

INT. FABULOUS FOX THEATRE AUDITORIUM - BACKSTAGE

Jazmyne is backstage and is looking at the crowd
trickling in.

                    JAZMYNE
          Good evening.

                    AUDIENCE
          Good evening.

                    JAZMYNE
          Welcome to the first annual
          Angels praise event, where the
          spirit of the Lord is lifted
          and his greatness is expressed.
          Expressed through dance. My
          name is Jazmyne Shepherd, the
          director of the program.
          Tonight you will be truly
          blessed with the spirit of
          dance. We have 15 girls with
          ages ranging from 5-15,
          different races, different
          walks of life. But they share
          one thing in common, a love
          for Christ. Without further
          ado, ladies and gentlemen,
          I present to you Angels…

Five little girls come out in ballerina outfits and
the music comes on. They begin to dance.

People continue to come in.

                    JAZMYNE
          (Talking to herself) Where are
          all of these people coming
          from? I don't understand.

Josh walks up behind her with a magazine in his
hand. He hands it to her and she's on the front.

                    JAZMYNE
          I don't get it. Where did they
          get this photo? I didn't do an
          interview with VIBE.

A reporter walks up to her.

                    REPORTER
          You didn't have to. Your
          husband answered all the
          questions I needed to know.

Jazmyne looks confused.

                    JAZMYNE
          You look familiar.

                    REPORTER
          I met you at...

                    JAZMYNE
          That's right. Look, I'm so
          sorry about how I treated you.

                    REPORTER
          No apology necessary. I see
          you've changed. You are doing
          bigger and better things.

                    JAZMYNE
        I see you are too!

                    JOSH
        He's the new associate editor
        at VIBE now.

                    REPORTER
        It's funny how God just works
        things out, huh? (pointing to
        the audience)

                    JAZMYNE
        Hmmm. (shaking head)

                    REPORTER
        I put a call out to all those
        folks who dissed you earlier.

Jazmyne continues to look at the audience and news
reporters begin showing up and setting up cameras.

                    REPORTER
        All I have to say is, this
        event has gained national
        attention. It's up to you now
        to represent correctly.

                    JAZMYNE
        (looks at Josh and then looks
        at the reporter) Thank you!
        (excited)

INT. TV STUDIO - LATE AFTERNOON

Al Smith

A television screen has the text "Live coverage" which then moves to two anchors sitting at a news desk. This program is being watched in many homes throughout the country.

INT. YADEH'S VIDEO SHOOT

There is a television set at the video shoot of Yadeh's next video. This news cast is being shown throughout various beauty salons and barber shops.

INT. YADEH'S VIDEO SET

Misha walks on the set with a robe on and approaches where the cameras are set up. Reshawn stares at her as she walks past. She is met by another woman who is in the position where she normally sits with Yadeh.

                    MISHA
          What's going on?

                    YADEH
          I ask the questions round here.
          Took you so long?

                    MISHA
          I had to…

                    YADEH
          Whatever, step aside—you're
          not in this scene.

                    MISHA
          What you mean? I'm in every
          scene.

                              YADEH
         Not today.

The other video vixen looks at Misha and then looks
away. She avoids eye contact. Misha walks off the
set in disgust and enters the holding area where
people are watching television. They are flipping
through the channels and they land on the channel
where Jazmyne's dance ministry is being televised.

INT. FABULOUS FOX THEATRE AUDITORIUM

Jazmyne walks back on stage after the five-year-olds
have performed.

                         JAZMYNE
              Those were our five-year-olds.
              They are so precious and
              innocent. So much innocence
              before being influenced by
              television and peer pressure.
              They are getting that
              foundation now. My grandfather
              always told me scripture:
              Teach them young and they will
              never depart from you. This
              ministry is set to reach young
              girls all the way to grown
              women. If someone out there
              wants to get it right, it's
              never too late. Allow God into
              your life. Usher Him in. He's
              just waiting for an invitation.

People continue to watch it in various places
throughout America.

Al Smith

INT. YADEH'S VIDEO SET - GREEN ROOM

Reshawn walks back to where Misha is sitting. He
signals for everyone to leave the immediate area
and he shuts the door.

                    RESHAWN
          You know what time it is.

He unbuckles his pants. Misha looks up at him with
a sad expression.

                    RESHAWN
          Yadeh said it's cool. Don't
          worry. Aight?

Misha is solemn. She's had to do this before with
other celebrities. She nods her head because she
understands that this is necessary. She kneels down
in front of him.

INT. STORE DRESSING ROOM - FLASHBACK

Jazmyne talking with Misha about Yadeh's behavior.

                    JAZMYNE
          I've been where you are. (cut
          to)He's gonna take your soul.
          He's not at peace. The constant
          nightmares he has. Times where
          he just seems where he's
          carrying the world on his
          shoulders. And he'll step on
          you in the process. (cut to)
          I was on a path of destruction.
          (cut to) But there's a better

JAZMYNE (Cont'd)
way.(cut to) I found Christ.

Misha gets up and attempts to walk out, but Reshawn
stops her.

RESHAWN
Where you think you goin'?

He attacks her and attempts to rape her.
People hear the commotion going on but no one
does anything.

INT. YADEH'S VIDEO SET

DIRECTOR
Cut! What in the hell is going
on back there? We are in the
middle of shooting.

Director is alarmed by the screaming and runs back
to where the noise is coming from and breaks up
the two.

DIRECTOR
Security! I heard about you.
(looking at Reshawn) Not on
my set.

Reshawn looks at the director but doesn't attempt
to fight with him. Misha regains her composure and
begins walking off of the set.

                    MISHA
          (Looking at the people on the
          set) No more. No more can I do
          this. You...You shouldn't do
          this. People are looking up to
          us...to you. (looking at Yadeh)
          For what? Because you're
          giving this image that you are
          "the man." No more. No more.
          We have to have some sort of
          conscience. We are being held
          accountable...to God. I can't do
          this anymore. I'm leaving.
          Anybody with me?

Misha looks around and proceeds walking.

                    YADEH
          You wasn't doin' anything no
          way. You done here.

Several people decide to leave with her.

                    YADEH
          Let'em leave.

Yadeh gets up and walks off the set.

INT. GREEN ROOM - MINUTES LATER

Yadeh is walking around and the television is
left on.

INT. ONE TELEVISION SCREEN IN GREEN ROOM

ANCHOR
We are reporting live from the
Fabulous Fox Theatre with the
Angels Dance Ministry brought
to you by Jazmyne Shepherd.
The event has just about a
sold out crowd with one group
left for the evening to
perform. I'm here with the
one and only Jazmyne Shepherd.
This is a wonderful show you
put on here.

JAZMYNE
Well, thank you so much, and I
hate to correct you, but this
is far from a show. It's a
ministry designed to reach out
to the young and old to share
the love of Christ. And I am
so proud of them. We have been
practicing all year for this
day, and I am so grateful.

Yadeh continues to watch.

ANCHOR
I apologize about that.

JAZMYNE
Oh no, you're fine, baby.

ANCHOR
So who do you have with you?

                    JAZMYNE
          This is my pastor, Pastor
          Sparks.

                    ANCHOR
          Good evening.

                 PASTOR SPARKS
          Evening.

                    ANCHOR
          How do you feel tonight is
          going?

                 PASTOR SPARKS
          I couldn't have asked for a
          better turnout. I am overjoyed
          with what Jazmyne has done
          with these girls. This sends
          a bold statement out to the
          community that they can be
          whatever they want to be.

INT. BACKSTAGE OF THE AUDITORIUM

The older girls are playing backstage and are
running in and out of the back door. A security
guard approaches them.

                 SECURITY GUARD
               Alright, ladies, everybody in.

The girls come inside.

SECURITY GUARD
        This door needs to be closed
        at all times. This leads to
        the alley. You don't want
        stray folks coming in here
        and taking one of you away,
        do you?

All of the girls shake their heads "no."

Camera trucks to Jazmyne standing behind the stage
waiting for her cue and proceeds on stage.

INT. YADEH'S VIDEO SHOOT GREEN ROOM - EVENING

Yadeh walks out in disgust after watching Jazmyne
on television.

INT. FABULOUS FOX THEATRE AUDITORIUM

The finale is wrapping up and the crowd is on their
feet with applause. They signal for Jazmyne to come
out on stage. They greet her with a bouquet of
flowers. They all bow. Jazmyne goes around and hugs
everyone on stage and goes down in the audience.
Jazmyne is surprised to see Misha in the audience.
They stare at each other for a moment. Misha begins
tearing and Jazmyne hugs her real tight.

INT. BACKSTAGE OF THE FOX THEATRE

CG: HOURS LATER

Al Smith

Everyone has left except for Jazmyne, Pastor
Sparks, Josh, and a handful of others. They are all
cleaning up. Josh is picking up trash throughout
the seats in the auditorium.

> PASTOR SPARKS
> What was done tonight was
> terrific and you… (looking at
> Natalie)…how were you able to
> get so high up in the air?

Everyone starts laughing. Josh walks up to
the group.

> JOSH
> You about ready? I'm a run
> this over to the dumpster.
> Be right back.

> JAZMYNE
> OK. (looking at girls) She did
> jump pretty high. That's from
> all that caffeine she had
> earlier.

Everyone laughs.

Josh walks to the back door and its wide open. Josh
stops and looks around and proceeds outside.

INT. BACKSTAGE OF THE FOX THEATRE

> PASTOR SPARKS
> Can you still get that high?

                    JAZMYNE
          Sure. (laughing)

EXT. DUMPSTER AREA BEHIND FOX THEATRE

Josh is dumping the trash.

INT. BACKSTAGE OF THE FOX THEATRE

                    SHULA
          I can get that high too. All
          she did was jump like this.

When Shula comes down, Yadeh appears in the
background.

Yadeh walks up to the group.

                    YADEH
          Don't stop on my account. I
          just came to get healed by the
          good reverend and this trick.
          Go ahead, Jazmyne, Reverend.
          Say something to save my soul.

                    JAZMYNE
          Yadeh, have you been here
          since the performance?

                    YADEH
          Long enough, enough to see
          what's a lie. So tell me, good
          reverend, have you told these
          outstanding citizens how you
          used to feel me up right
          before bedtime every night?

Al Smith

Pastor Sparks sighs.

> YADEH
>
> Did you?

> PASTOR SPARKS
>
> Yes, I did.

> YADEH
>
> How you broke up our family?
> How you kicked me out the
> house?

> PASTOR SPARKS
>
> Yes, I told them, son.

> YADEH
>
> Don't call me son. I ain't
> your son. Your son died long
> time ago. You killed that
> innocent little boy.

> PASTOR SPARKS
>
> Not a day has gone by that I
> haven't thought about that.
> I've begged the Lord to
> forgive me. I'm a changed man.

> YADEH
>
> Yeah, well, I don't forgive
> you.

> PASTOR SPARKS
>
> I hope that one day you will.

                    YADEH
Not today. (pulls out a gun)

                    JAZMYNE
Why not? I forgave you. You
hurt me bad. All the pain and
agony you've caused me. If I
don't forgive you, then God
won't forgive me of the wrong
I've done. Put the gun down.

                    YADEH
So the good reverend's got you
brainwashed, huh? So let me
get this right: You a prayin'
man, huh? You a changed man?
You a God fearing man? You
believe you going to heaven?

Pastor nods his head.

                    YADEH
Well today is your lucky day.
You get to meet him.

Pastor Sparks jumps at Yadeh and manages to get
a hold of the gun. They begin to wrestle. The gun
goes off once in the air. It goes off a second time.
Then it goes off again and people start
crying. They stop fighting. Pastor Sparks runs
over to Jazmyne. She's shot in the chest and is
lying on the ground. Yadeh gets up and looks
around in disbelief. He shoots himself and falls
to the ground.

Al Smith

Josh hears the commotion and runs back inside the
building. He runs into the auditorium and sees
Yadeh and Jazmyne laying on the floor bleeding.

INT. HOSPITAL WAITING ROOM - HOURS LATER

The waiting room is filled with people, ranging from
little ballerinas to hip hop fans to see Yadeh.

The doctor comes out and signals for Josh to come
over to where he is standing.

                    DOCTOR
          We were able to save the baby.
          She's gonna be just fine.

                    JOSH
          She? A little girl? And
          Jazmyne?

                    DOCTOR
          There was too much blood loss.
          I'm sorry.

                    JOSH
          What do you mean?

                    DOCTOR
          We weren't able to save her.

Josh falls down and sits on the floor with his head
in his hands and begins weeping.

The camera pans to another hospital room where
there are an abundance of hip hop supporters
waiting to see the condition of Yadeh.

Pastor Sparks is sitting in the hospital room with Yadeh.

Fades to black.

[Sound effects of camera flashes and new announcers]

EXT. HOSPITAL FRONT ENTRANCE

              NEWS ANCHOR
        We have just arrived on the
        scene of a murder and suicide
        attempt that happened late
        last night, and although
        details are very sketchy,
        what we do know is two of the
        victims are recording artist
        Yadeh Ya and video vixen
        Jazmyne Greer. Evidently words
        had been exchanged and gunfire
        took place here at the
        Fabulous Fox Theatre…

The camera pans to another news crew and the reporter is speaking in Spanish. The camera continues to pan throughout the crowd and captures yet another camera crew, and this reporter is speaking in Japanese. Out of all of the languages spoken, the only words that all of them share is "Yadeh Ya" and "Jazmyne Greer."

              PAPA'S V.O.
        At this moment in time, this
        very hour, we say farewell to
        America's beautiful brown
        butterfly. Her years will be

                PAPA'S V.O. (cont'd)
cherished. Her life will be
celebrated. Never for a moment
will we imagine a life without
her existence. Many viewed her
as a legend, destined to lead
the next generation of little
girls from a self-destructive
path to a passion for Christ.
From deep within the five
boroughs to the heart of fifth
ward, she will be deeply
missed. She had a way of
reaching and touching your
heart. Have you ever spoken to
Jazmyne? Has she ever smiled
at you? If you have, you know
that she was genuine. And her
place in this world will never
be filled. Her existence will
be recorded in the journals of
the bewildered and the saved,
as a witness of Christ. To
others she was known as wife,
daughter, friend, Christian.
The words for my granddaughter
tickle my tongue as I smile
and speak about the time and
space we briefly shared on this
earth. Now the hour has come
for us to be reunited once
more. Jazmyne, my child,
welcome to eternal life.

(Montage of pictures)

- Jazmyne posing in front of the camera (at the beginning of the movie)

- Fist fight when she and Josh were in elementary school

- Jazmyne holding a butterfly (at 13)

- Jazmyne and Papa in an open field

- Jazmyne and Josh practicing for a high school talent show

- Dancing in the ballet

- Jazmyne at Papa's funeral

- Jazmyne teaching young girls how to ballet

- Jazmyne laughing

- Jazmyne receiving her GED

- Jazmyne crying in Josh's hospital room

- Josh and Jazmyne's wedding picture

- Jazmyne's body being buried at a cemetery

INT. BOOKSTORE CAFE - TWO YEARS LATER

Al Smith

The scene fades in with Josh sitting inside of a
bookstore. He is signing autographs in his photo
journal. Josh looks a little older. He has a
full beard.

                    JOSH
        And who do I make this out to?

He is talking to a young pre-teen who is sort
of bashful.
                YOUNG GIRL
        Shalena.

                    JOSH
        "To my favorite little
        bookworm, grow and fly. Josh.
        " How's that?

                YOUNG GIRL
        Thank you.

Josh closes the book to reveal the cover: The title
of the book is The Life and Times of Jazmyne Greer

- A Photographic Journey.

Josh looks down at a two-year-old girl.

                  JOSH
        Ready to go?

The little girl smiles. The camera pans down to her
hands. She is holding an empty glass jar.

Fades to black.

www.ingramcontent.com/pod-product-compliance
Lightning Source LLC
Chambersburg PA
CBHW030330030726
47499CB00003B/709